Dream Glasses

Book 1 of the Rosethorn Series

Dream Glasses

Geri —
Let The Dream Glasses take you
away — and enjoy the journey!

Linda L Flynn

Linda L Flynn

***journeytotheheights*.com**

This book is a work of fiction. Names, characters, places and incidents are the product of the author's imagination or used fictionally. Any resemblance to actual persons, living or dead, or to actual events is coincidental. The descriptions of locations in Paris, France are designed to make the reader feel at home in the neighborhood. Any activities taken place in these locations are fictional.

ISBN-10: 1541058151
ISBN-13: 978-1541058156

For all the dreamers in the world.
May you find the path to your dream.

TABLE OF CONTENTS

ACKNOWLEDGMENTS

Dream Glasses is a fictional work, which began with a fun writing prompt one day. The story evolved, and the characters took on their own lives. While laying words on paper, I found commonality in the longing to search for a dream. My dream was different, but still a journey.

No good work can be accomplished alone. I owe many people heartfelt thanks for their support and encouragement. I'm indebted to the following people:

My mom, for the countless hours she spent reading me stories when I was young, which instilled a love for the printed word. That love gave birth to the dream of someday writing.

Thanks to the people who imparted an interest in travel and understanding of different cultures. Travel and foreign culture are loves that permeate my life.

The Carbondale Writer's group, their support and encouragement kept me focused.

For the early readers, who encouraged me to continue with the story and pointed out necessary corrections.

To Corrie Karnan, Jill Sheeley and Maria Yurasek with whom I formed a bond after taking a publishing class at our local college. We've become friends and encouragers and have done the hard work of editing; suggesting changes that sometime stretch one into being a better writer. I look forward to working with each of you on future projects.

To you, my readers for validating my dream of writing!

Special thanks to my husband Tom, who believed in my writing when I still considered 'writing' as 'a dream.' There is little he allows to stand in the way of my writing times. His steady encouragement, loving understanding and help are essential to me. To him I give my deepest gratitude and devotion.

Chapter I

With her head high and her back erect, Liz hurried to work early this fall morning. She stopped at the coffee machine then headed to her office. Already she imagined the orange scent and herself savoring the flavor as the cookie dissolved in her mouth. She rounded the corner, stopped and just stood there staring at her desk.

"What? There's no cookie!"

In the location where she'd been finding these delicious orange flavored cookies was a small envelope propped against her penholder. The handwriting was unfamiliar. It was a delicate calligraphy script in black ink.

"What the heck? I didn't eat breakfast and was looking forward to my morning treat."

Liz slowly reached out, picked up the envelope and glimpsed around the office before tearing the flap open.

The inside sheet contained the same lacey delicate handwriting.

"I hope you've been enjoying the cookies. I'd love to share the recipe with you. I thought we could meet after work. I'll be at the coffee house on the corner of 7th and Clarke today at 4:30. You'll be able to find me by the plate of cookies on the table. I'm excited to share the cookies with you in person. See you then."

Liz looked around the office to see if anyone was watching as she read the note. All the early crew appeared to be engrossed in their own tasks. While she pondered who wrote this note, Eric, her boss, walked up behind her.

"Liz, what's the matter? Are you all right? You look like you've just seen a ghost."

Before Liz could respond, Eric continued.

"Don't you have a project to be working on?"

"Oh. Oh, yes. I'll get right on the Dream Glasses project. I was just trying to figure out something that happened this morning," Liz said.

Eric laid his head back and laughed.

"Hasn't something strange been happening every morning for several months?"

Liz shrugged and Eric continued.

"I walk around the office most days before the staff arrive. I've noticed your desk is the only one with a cookie waiting every morning. At first I assumed you were leaving one on your desk before you left for the day so it would be waiting for you when you arrived in the morning. Then I realized that is too strange. I noticed there's no cookie today. So who's been leaving you the treats? Who's the secret admirer?"

Liz sighed.

"I don't know. At first I thought it strange. Somehow they seem familiar, but I can't remember why. Honestly, they are the best cookies I've ever eaten. This morning I was disappointed to find 'no cookie'. There was a note in its place; the person wants to meet. And I still can't identify who's been leaving them."

"So, what've you decided?" said Eric.

"I don't know. The project needs a few finishing touches before tomorrow's presentation."

Liz sat down at her desk.

"Talk with you later," said Eric.

The project excited Liz. She remembered how it all started. Struthers and Sloan were resistant to Redesign You. Liz, bored with her job was trying to figure how she could find something else to do. Redesign You came along with their Dream Glasses, suggesting they would allow one to envision their true potential. Liz wanted the glasses to work hoping they would point her to a new career. She promoted the project to management and they assigned the task to her. Secretly, she was thrilled to be assigned the project. Redesign You left her a pair of glasses to test out while working on the evaluation. Several of her co-workers thought it was a joke and often poked fun at her as they passed her desk. The glasses were odd looking, and she didn't want her co-workers to see her wearing them, consequently she took them home.

One evening as she sat on the couch, she reached over, picked up the glasses and put them on. Everything appeared fuzzy at first, and then came into focus. Liz found herself in the middle of a large group of people. They praised her for creating these amazing desserts. As she looked around there were plates of various tempting pastries. The fragrances were those of freshly baked goods.

She brushed her hair back and touched the glasses. Then thought that's odd, I don't wear glasses. She took them off and found she was back in her living room, sitting on the couch.

The next time she put them on she saw herself in a baker's kitchen, complete with every tool imaginable. She mixed things together and stopped to make notes on a notepad. Each time she took the glasses off, she was back in her normal environment.

These dreams of being a successful baker stayed with Liz. She felt something unexplainable stir deep in her spirit. She remembered the many hours she spent in the kitchen with her grandmother and all the delectable treats they used to make. Those were happy times where Liz had fun, much more fun than she experienced working in product research and development. The longer she worked on this project, the more she determined she would leave Struthers and Sloan. She was waiting for the right time. Liz questioned how she could pursue this baking passion when the cookies showed up on her desk.

Today the note appeared. She wondered if this was the opportunity she'd been waiting for. Could she leave the corporate world behind, be successful and happy doing something else?

By mid-afternoon, with the presentation completed, Liz realized she'd decided. She packed up her laptop and a notepad, gathered her purse and jacket then headed for the door.

Eric approached her as she was leaving.

"It looks like you're on a mission. I guess that means you will meet the 'cookie person.' Do you think it's a good idea to go by yourself?"

"It's 4 in the afternoon. I'm going to the Tantalizing Bean. Doesn't that sound safe enough?"

"I have to admit, it sounds safe. But I'd like to check with you in about 45 minutes–and maybe later. Would you mind?" said Eric.

Liz nodded in agreement.

"I guess that's okay. See you tomorrow."

She left the office, rounded the corner and observed the Tantalizing Bean. Liz came here often, but this time was different. She took a deep breath and the rich aroma of coffee filled her lungs as she peered through the shop windows. Nothing looked abnormal or out of place. It was just a coffee shop.

She stamped her foot and thought to herself, No! It's not *just* a coffee shop. This is where my friends and I come to relax. I love being here. Is it odd, this mystery person picked one of my favorite places?

A group of people sat at one table with their heads together in deep conversation. Singles worked away on their laptops and others sat engrossed in books they were reading. Suddenly Liz observed a plate of familiar cookies on a table. The table, flanked by several overstuffed chairs hosted someone sitting with their back to the window. Only the back of a floppy wide brimmed hat was visible.

Darn! Still no idea who I'm meeting, but at least it appears to be a woman thought Liz. She sighed, took another deep breath, stood tall and pulled open the door to the coffee shop. The familiar fragrance of dark rich coffee greeted her and immediately made her feel at home. She headed straight to the table with the cookies.

The woman was reading a foreign fashion magazine. She was tall and slender. Wearing a black sheath dress with large but simple jewelry; her dark hair was pulled back in low twist at her neckline; she was stylish. As Liz approached she could see the woman was wearing oversized sunglasses and still engrossed in her magazine. Liz cleared her throat; the woman glanced up and removed her sunglasses.

"Darlin', you haven't changed one bit."

"Sabine! What are you doing here?"

Liz was back at college graduation. Back when Sabine announced she and my boyfriend Bill were going to France to meet Sabine's parents. All those feelings of betrayal and hurt came flooding back. Liz was struggling with her memories from those college days when Sabine broke the silence.

"Liz, please sit down. I didn't know if you'd come or not."

Liz sat down in the comfy chair while Sabine continued.

"My parents recently passed away and left me the family business. I've been wondering what to do and couldn't stop thinking of you. I know things ended poorly between us and it was my fault. I didn't know it then, but Bill was a self-centered womanizer whose only priority was Bill. Last I heard he was on his fourth wife. Can we forget the past and talk about now?"

Sabine sat there and waited for Liz to say something. Liz sank back into the oversized chair facing Sabine and reflected on some of the fun times they'd had in college. Going back to the days of easy banter between them, and the girl jokes shared at the day's end would be nice. But can I trust her? All those feelings I believed were behind me. They sure rushed back when she was right in front of me. How do I forgive Sabine for hurting me the way she did?

Liz sat and smiled at Sabine.

Sabine ordered drinks for them and sat there for a moment as she eyed Liz up and down.

"Wow. You've gone all out for the career woman style. That's a beautiful suit. The matching tote and heels offer a nice finishing touch. What are you doing these days?"

Liz observed the cookies on the table, but didn't feel comfortable helping herself.

Sabine pushed the plate of cookies towards her.

"Help yourself. I remember how much you loved my mother's Madeleines. In fact, remembering that is why I'm here. I suspect you are staying out of curiosity. You're wondering why I would contact you after all these years."

"That's why the flavor seemed familiar. We haven't seen each other in probably ten years. I forgot about the Madeleines. I loved those cookies but didn't remember having them before. I work in product research and development at Struthers and Sloan. Right now there's another company trying to sell us the rights to one of their products. I'm conducting the preliminary research. I suppose I enjoy my job. What've you been up to?" said Liz.

"What do you mean, you suppose you enjoy your job? I always expected you would do what you wanted. You're smart and determined," said Sabine.

Sabine paused again and then continued.

"After graduation, I headed back to France. My parents wanted me to learn the family business and take it to the next level. I planned for Bill and I to be a team; he would guide me in the business. My folks were happy the day he left. I couldn't get my head around the business, but not for lack of trying. The truth is my parents weren't comfortable turning the business over to me. Instead of retiring, they kept on working, trying to mentor me. They were hoping I would learn the ropes. I was trying. I mastered the baking and got interested in the business end of things. Last winter they both died in a tragic head-on car crash on the way home from a ski holiday. Since their deaths, I've been struggling to keep things going; wondering how long I can do this. I kept thinking of you. Your love of these cookies, your head for business and your determination to accomplish anything you set your mind to were things I remembered about you. I realized I had to find you. But I was nervous. I finally figured out where you worked and then found an old contact working in your building's housekeeping department. For a fee, they agreed to leave a daily cookie on your desk. I would send them over weekly until I decided try to meet with you. Now here I am. You weren't an easy person to find."

Liz burst out laughing, Sabine had changed little. Liz glanced up just as Eric rushed into the coffee shop. He looked around. It was clear he was looking for someone. His eyes locked on Liz and he headed toward her.

"Hi there. Wow. You look like you have some delicious snacks. Are you going to introduce me to your friend?"

He rested his hand on Liz's shoulder.

Sabine scoped out Eric and started beaming.

"Wow, Liz. If he's your friend when are you going to introduce us? Otherwise…"

Before Sabine could continue, Liz stood up and locked arms with Eric.

"This is one of my co-workers. He's my boss and one of my best friends. Sabine, I would like you to meet Eric. Eric this is Sabine. We went to college together and then lost touch with one another after she returned to France. Today is rather a surprise, meeting with her."

Liz pulled up a chair close to hers for Eric. As he sat down, Liz noticed the fragrance of his aftershave and wondered why she had never noticed this before?

Eric glanced at the large plate of cookies. He didn't know if he smelled the treats on the table or the coffee shop pastries, but they sure looked good.

"Would you like to try one of these cookies or order something to drink first?" said Sabine.

"I'll just wait for my coffee."

All talking ceased; everyone seemed to notice the silence and sensed awkwardness.

Eric said, "Did I interrupt something? Would you like me to leave?"

Sabine quickly responded, "Of course not. If you're a friend of Liz, you should stay. We haven't seen each other in years, and I must admit, it's my fault we didn't stay in touch with each other. I'm hoping we can correct that and rebuild our friendship. In fact, I'm hoping I can tempt her to return to Paris with me."

Liz gasped.

Eric couldn't decide whose reaction to watch first.

"You do mean for a vacation, right?"

Sabine hesitated.

"No, but this isn't how I intended to ask you. Liz, I'd like you to come to Paris and help me run the bakery. Please, would you at least agree to consider this? We can talk about the details after you've entertained the idea. It would be great fun. And Paris is a wonderful city. We used to have such good times together."

"Really? Sabine, I haven't seen you in years. I'm in the middle of a huge project. I have to present my initial findings to management tomorrow. I need to stay focused for this meeting. Can I get your number? I'll call you in a day or two. We can sit down and talk then. I can't think about anything except my project right now. I hope you don't mind if I call it a day, but I should get going."

Surprised by Liz's response, Sabine hesitated.

"Sure. I'm at the Carlton. Here's the number – I'm in room 212. I'll be waiting for your call."

Sabine pulled a hotel card from her purse and thrust it at Liz.

"Please call! I want to mend our friendship and talk about this offer. Oh, and good luck on your meeting tomorrow. I'm sure you'll WOW them."

Liz glanced at the card as she picked it up and dropped it into her purse. She stood and gathered her things.

"Thanks Sabine. I'll be okay after tomorrow. We should be able to talk after I'm done with the presentation. It's good to see you again, and it'll be fun to hear what you are trying to cook up now. You're always involved in something."

Eric stood.

"Can I accompany you?"

Sabine smiled at Eric.

"You don't have to leave yet do you? You haven't even tried one cookie. These are the cookies I was leaving for Liz."

Liz shook her head, turned and looked over her shoulder.

"I'll see you tomorrow in the office. Everything's under control and I want you available for support. Have a good time. Don't forget to try one of those cookies. They're the best!"

"OK, if you're sure. They certainly look good."

Eric slid back into his chair.

As Liz headed for the door she remembered again how Sabine acted with her and thought she hasn't changed much. Does she think I'll just drop everything and come to Paris? I have to stay focused. Tomorrow's meeting is important!

Sabine smiled as Eric sat back down.

"Oh, I'm confident you'll enjoy them. Have you known Liz for long?"

"Hmmm. Liz and I started at the company the same week. We went through all the introductory programs together and just seemed to hit it off. We both have this quirky sense of humor and I'm sure she'll convince management to continue on with phase two of the Dream Glasses project. That's the project Liz is working on right now. I can't wait to hear her presentation tomorrow. I'm glad she wants me to be there."

Eric was savoring the small cookie he'd picked up.

"Say, I like the orange flavor. Is that what makes them so special?"

Sabine studied Eric's reaction to the taste of the cookies.

"There's orange in the cookies. It is an old recipe from my grandmother's family. They're Madeleines. When in college, my mother would always include them in any package she sent me. It surprised me Liz didn't remember eating them while studying for finals. Did you know she was finding cookies on her desk?"

Eric nodded yes and Sabine continued.

"Didn't she have any idea where they were coming from? She looked startled when she saw me today. Where else did she expect they would come from?"

Eric took a sip of his coffee and paused for a moment.

"I knew she was receiving the cookies, but we never talked about it until today. This morning, she was disappointed to find a note instead of a cookie. She may have wondered at first who was leaving the cookies, but I believe she enjoyed them so much she stopped wondering where they came from. Did she tell you about the project she's working on? She's fixated on it. We weren't sure we wanted to take on this project, but Liz believed it would be a great challenge and told us it would be important for Struthers and Sloan. So we said yes to Redesign You. Liz is an amazing woman! If you shared cookies while in college, were you in the same classes?"

"We shared a dorm room together and had a few business classes together. I supposed she might have told you about her college days. Take another cookie."

Sabine didn't want Eric to leave; she picked up the plate and held it while Eric selected another cookie.

"No, Liz hasn't talked about her college days. I'm sure the company verified her records but at Struthers and Sloan, once you're hired it's rare anyone talks about your past. They're concerned about your current accomplishments."

Eric finished the cookie and the rest of his coffee.

"Sabine, it's been a pleasure to meet you. I hope we'll see more of you. I should get going. Tomorrow will be big day."

"Do you think Liz will contact me? Or have I wasted my time coming to America?"

Sabine's expectancy was evident.

"Liz is a solid person. She told you she'd get back in touch with you and I'm sure she will. Let her get through this presentation and the outcome of it before expecting to hear from her. She's focused when involved in something."

Eric stood to leave and held out his hand.

"It's been a pleasure. And thanks for the cookies. This is a flavor I won't be forgetting soon."

Sabine shook his hand. She watched as Eric walked out of the café. She wondered how she was going to keep herself busy for the next couple of days.

Chapter II

Liz arrived home. Unable to decide if meeting Sabine sealed her fate in corporate work or if it was her ticket to freedom, she sank into the couch. Unconsciously, she picked up the Dream Glasses and turned them over in her hands. Hungry, she headed to the kitchen and set the glasses on the counter. Hunting through the refrigerator, she found hummus and fresh vegetables and sat at the bar. Wondering if the glasses would guide her in what to do, she reached over and slipped them on her face.

Liz found herself engulfed in the fragrance of baking bread, in a commercial kitchen. A tray of small fruit tarts was right in front of her. They looked perfect; mounded with bright red raspberries and soft swirls of whipped cream, they were ready to serve. The doorbell rang. Liz shook her head and stood to open the door.

Eric stood there.

"Hi Liz. You wear glasses?"

Liz slipped the glasses from her face.

"Oh, I forgot I had them on. I don't wear glasses."

"Really? Why are they on your face?"

"Eric! These are the Dream Glasses. I brought a pair home when I started the project. I figured I'd have more opportunities to determine how they worked. The project has come together well."

Liz slid the glasses into her pocket.

"I imagine you want to discuss the project?"

Liz held the door open and Eric entered. He glanced around her condo.

"I never realized you liked contemporary decorating. This is a nice place! I've never been here. We've always met at a café or pub around town. I love the view and can see why you're contented here. Are you ready for tomorrow?"

Liz motioned for Eric to take a seat.

"Sure. Why? This is the first time, you've shown concern about one of my management presentations."

"Well, the way you rushed out of the coffee house concerned me. I'm checking to make sure you're ok. Perhaps it's silly of me, but here I am. You don't mind, do you?" said Eric.

"I guess I did kinda rush out. Sabine startled me. I haven't thought of her in years. It confounded me to find she was the one leaving the cookies. The flavor seemed familiar, but I couldn't remember why. After the first couple of days, I stopped caring. They were sooo good; they were my morning treat. We parted with many unresolved issues, for her to just show up and say she wanted me to return with her to Paris was more than I could comprehend today. I can't fathom if I'd have gone to the café knowing Sabine was there. We shared some good times in college. Yet, drama follows her. I'm in a different place now. I didn't mean to be rude and didn't intend to leave you there on your own. Hope you didn't mind."

"Wow! When I arrived, you guys appeared to be two old friends. I'm not sure what to say. Do you want to grab a bite to eat? I hear there's a new cafe around the corner, with live music. Would getting out help you clear your mind and relax?" Eric said.

Liz hesitated for a moment.

"Thanks Eric! Another evening and I'd say yes. But tonight I want to relax here at home. I have things to consider. Want to join me for an early coffee before the Dream Glasses meeting?"

"Sure. Meet you tomorrow," said Eric.

As he headed for the door, he turned and studied Liz.

"Are you going to be okay tonight?"

"You bet. See you tomorrow morning."

Liz shut the door behind Eric and leaned against it. Her thoughts raced between Paris and Eric. Now it looked like there might be two options in her life.

Liz walked back to the kitchen where she poured herself a glass of wine; sat in her favorite chair and picked up the most recent *Food and Wine* magazine.

Chapter III

At the office, the next morning Eric waited for Liz at her desk with a big smile, two steaming lattes and a pastry bag.

"You look great, like you're ready for anything today! Let's enjoy this light breakfast and get ready to 'go get'em'! I've got the conference room all set up for you. You bring your lap top; everything else is prepared for the meeting."

"Thanks! The coffee smells great!"

Liz grabbed a cup and stopped to savor the aroma.

"Hey this coffee is hazelnut, isn't it? How'd you know it's my favorite?"

Liz closed her eyes and smiled as she enjoyed the first swallow.

"Mmmmm… This coffee is delicious! I feel like I could conquer the world today. Are you ready?"

She smiled at Eric as she turned and headed to the conference room.

Eric picked up the pastry bag and followed Liz.

"Don't you want to know what I brought from the bakery?"

The meeting was successful. Management was intrigued by the presentation. The VP questioned how this could be real and stated he still had some reservations. The executives voted and determined they wanted to move forward with phase two of the product research. Liz knew the drill. She would turn the project over to the next team. Satisfied with the impact of her presentation and management's reaction, she returned to her office space. Surprised to hear of management's excitement over the Dream Glasses some of her co-workers stopped by to ask how she knew this project would be impressive. Some grumbled as they walked away because it was Liz's success of the day, not theirs.

Eric said, "I knew you'd impress them today. Do you want to share what the secret is to Dream Glasses?"

Liz said, "You were in the meeting! The glasses show the wearer new potentials or possibilities for their life. I believe the glasses allow people to see their potential and allow them to unlock hidden sides of their personality."

Liz considered the day a success. She was still smiling when she arrived home.

She couldn't shake the exhilarating feelings she experienced whenever she pondered Sabine's offer. Still struggling with what to say to Sabine, she called the hotel.

Sabine was out, so Liz left a message at the front desk asking Sabine to meet again at the coffee shop after work on Monday. Liz sighed, put the phone down and realized she had a few more days before she talked to Sabine.

Liz slept late on Saturday morning and then headed to the park for a long walk to clear her mind. She knew she had to forgive Sabine if she was going to Paris. Her cell rang; she saw it was Eric and took the call.

"Hey Liz. What are you doing? Want to meet for lunch at the Bistro? What do you say?"

"That sounds great! I'm at the park, walking. It'll take me about 40 minutes to get to the Bistro."

"I'll come get you."

Liz said, "I need the exercise! I'll walk and meet you there in less than an hour."

"OK, I'll see you there and have a table waiting for us. Bye."

"Bye".

Liz stood in the park wondering why Eric wanted to meet on a Saturday. She didn't know, but she was glad he called. Picking up the pace, she headed to the Bistro.

The Bistro was another of Liz's favorite places! Delectable scents filled the air. There were few empty tables, but the atmosphere was quiet. European décor with low lighting greeted one when they walked in the door.

Eric sat at a table in the corner. He waved the minute Liz walked in the door. He stood as Liz approached.

"You look great today! Thanks for agreeing to meet me on such short notice. Have a seat and get comfortable. I ordered a soda for you. Hope you don't mind."

Liz sat down.

"That's great! Thanks. And thanks for suggesting lunch."

"You were a hit yesterday with the Dream Glasses campaign. How did you develop the ideas for the presentation? It sounded like you were selling the idea you should leave Struthers and Sloan."

Liz lowered her voice and leaned forward.

"Remember when I asked for a pair of the glasses? Originally I considered the entire project cheesy. I figured Redesign You was trying to regain their costs on a failed project and I wanted to expose them. I guess I also was curious enough to see if I could find some direction. I wanted to give the project a try. I had things I needed to find out. Well, after I put the glasses on, I couldn't believe what happened. In fact, I forgot I had them on. I was someplace different and I saw dreams or passions just like they were happening."

"Wow! Well you did a super job. Now what are you going to do concerning Sabine?"

18

Eric looked relaxed in his chair. The waiter brought their drinks to the table.

Liz took a deep breath.

"I haven't decided what I'll tell her. You know, I've been questioning if research and development is how I want to spend the rest of my life? I've envisioning myself running a bakery! Before I give her an answer, I need more information."

Eric gulped.

"I thought you liked your job at Struthers and Sloan. You did a super job presenting the ideas for the Dream Glasses! You were meticulous. And…and I can't imagine working there with you being gone. Promise me you won't commit to Sabine until you and I talk again. Promise?"

Liz's head was spinning. How much should she tell Eric?

"Ok. You need to know the Dream Glasses play a big part in the reason I'm excited about Sabine's offer. She and I ended on a sour note. But, I need a career change. I know it's sudden. I need a better understanding of what she's offering and what she wants from me."

"The Dream Glasses! They've really gotten under your skin. Do you believe they'll impact the public, or were you launching an idea?"

"Eric, you don't understand what those glasses unlock! Maybe I'm being silly, but they helped reveal my dream. I locked it up because it didn't seem practical or profitable. I didn't want to disappoint my father again. I have to listen to Sabine's offer. I'm meeting with her Monday after work. Let's talk after I meet with her, ok?"

"Ok."

Eric took the cue. They didn't discuss Sabine again. They finished their lunches, discussed work and upcoming cultural events at the civic center. It was a lovely afternoon. Liz realized she was sad it was coming to an end.

"I'll walk you home before I head over to the gym," said Eric.

"I'd love that!"

They headed for the door and walked into the sunshine and fresh air.

Chapter IV

At work on Monday, Liz accomplished little. Her mind kept wandering to her meeting with Sabine, the offer and what it might mean for her. She wondered if she would absolutely quit her job? I love the people I work with, but I don't want to spend my entire life stuck in this office. Why does baking seem authentic when I have those Dream Glasses on? What does that mean? What if I say 'yes' to Liz, get to Paris and find I hate it? Then what? Her mind raced with questions and she couldn't focus. Finally the day ended. She packed up her briefcase and headed for the door.

Eric caught up with Liz just as she was leaving.

"You look serious! You're meeting with Sabine and I hope it goes well. Remember, you agreed to talk with me before you commit to anything. I look forward to talking with you later. OK?"

Liz looked into Eric's eyes and could see his concern.

"Yes, I'll call you later tonight."

Eric shook his head.

"No let's meet at the Bistro for dinner. It's one of your favorite places. You'll be able to relax there and we can talk."

"OK, I'll see you then. Thanks!"

Liz headed out the door.

As she approached the coffee house, the door was open and the aroma of fresh coffee wafted through the air. Excitement filled the room as people talked and laughed at various tables. Sabine had a plate of cookies on the table. Papers lay fanned out in front of her. Liz entered and Sabine beamed the minute she saw her.

"Hi Liz. It's great to see you! I ordered a latte for you."

"Thanks! You brought another plate of those delicious cookies."

Liz didn't wait for an offer; she took a cookie from the plate as she sank into the oversized chair. The waiter was heading to the table with a steaming latte.

Liz felt Sabine studying her.

"I'm delighted you came! I didn't mean to spring my plans on you the way I did the last time we met. It was uncomfortable for you. That's not how I wanted our conversation to go. Mother and father died leaving me the Blé Sucré. It's a wonderful bakery, but I'm inept at business things. I can't tell if we'll make it or not. I could use your help! I'd like to make you a partner in the business, but would settle for you coming over for a few months to help me get things in order. Will you at least consider my offer? Otherwise, I have no one else to turn to. The people in Paris who could help me would rather the business fail. My parents ran such a successful bakery, it has become a threat to many other bakers."

Liz glanced at some of the papers Sabine had pushed towards her. Sabine observed the frown on Liz's face.

"I knew if anyone could make sense out of these accounts, it would be you! Do you think you can save the business? No! I mean, will you help me save the business?"

Liz sat there looking over the numbers. She immediately wondered where the profits were going? Sales appeared high, margins too. Something must be going on.

"Sabine, I don't know if I can solve your problems or not. The numbers don't look right, but I'd need more information.

Even then, I might find nothing. I've been pondering a career change, and I've been thinking about baking. If I come to Paris, can I apprentice in the bakery?"

"Yes, of course you can! It doesn't make sense to be at a bakery without baking. You'll be baking!"

"I'm not ready to commit to being a partner, but I'd love to come to Paris, to work in your bakery and help you make the bakery profitable."

"Are you sure? That's wonderful! I'm booked to return to Paris tomorrow evening. Once I'm home, I'll start the paperwork for your work permit. You must provide me with the dates of your flights both ways. I thought you might be more comfortable starting out with a temporary arrangement. We can see how things go. I'll set you up for a 90-day work permit, and you should apply for a 6-month visa. That'll give you time to evaluate life in Paris and avoid some of the paperwork and language evaluations of a longer visa. If you decide you want to stay, I'll start the paperwork for a longer permit and you can submit for an extended work visa."

"Were you counting on my coming? It sounds like you've already worked out many of the details of your request and the work required from both of us, just to get me there." Liz said.

"Well…yes! I was counting on you coming. Without your help, I worry that the business may not succeed. I researched what my request entailed. Coming over to work for 90 days is uncomplicated as long as I file all the correct paperwork. You can stay for six months, but only work for 90 days. You'll need a physical and proof of health insurance with some specific coverage. Don't worry about the details. I'll email all that information to you. Coming over longer has additional requirements and paperwork. You would have to take language proficiency tests to ensure you'll assimilate into the culture. If you don't pass the examinations, you're required to take language classes. I figured you'd want to assess Paris before making a permanent change and I need to get the business turned around. I hope my plan makes sense to you."

For a moment Liz was quiet.

"I guess I didn't realize all that's involved. I must find someone to lease my condo. I'll get started on my paperwork here, determine what I'm bringing and get my place ready to rent out. I can hardly believe I'll be coming to Paris."

"Me either. Expect the paperwork soon. I can't wait to have you in Paris!" said Sabine.

Leaving the coffee shop Liz headed to the Bistro to meet Eric. He was sitting at a table in the back corner.

"Hi, Liz. I wondered where you were! How did things go?"

Breathless, Liz slid into the bench.

"I'm fascinated! I glanced at some of the numbers and they don't seem correct. Sabine agreed I could apprentice in the bakery while trying to help solve the problem. Living in Paris will be exhilarating."

Eric leaned in.

"So, you're considering moving to Paris? What about Struthers and Sloan? Do you suspect someone is stealing from her? If you solved the problem would be you be able to help her make the business profitable again? Your presentation yesterday was about you, wasn't it? What's this fantasy about baking?"

Eric sat back and gazed at Liz waiting for her response.

Liz took a breath.

"Where to start? Yes, I surmise someone is stealing from her. Something is going on. It might be someone stealing cash, stealing supplies or overcharging and under delivering supplies. But the numbers don't seem right. My fantasy with baking…"

Liz paused. How much should she reveal about the Dream Glasses and what happened when she put them on? Eric just sat there, absentmindedly stirring his coffee and waiting for a response.

"You've watched me get all excited about Redesign You. I took a pair of Dream Glasses home to prove they were phony. I didn't expect what happened! With the glasses on, I thought I was living a different life. I was an amazing baker and people were clamoring for my pastries. The fragrant aromas from baking pastries filled the room. I was in the middle of a large professional kitchen with every imaginable tool available. When I bushed my hair out of my face, I touched the glasses. The moment I realized I don't wear glasses and took them off the images left and I was sitting on my couch. I've put them on twice and each time, I see images of me being a successful baker. I've become more and more excited about the possibility of running a bakery. Then Sabine shows up with this offer. Can I help her make her business profitable again, or do I just want to test this fantasy of being a baker? I can't say no to her. I may not get another opportunity to determine if baking is for me! I'll stay at Struthers and Sloan until Sabine and I have all the paperwork submitted; find someone to lease my condo; and get everything in order. Then I have to leave. Even if baking isn't right for me, I know research and development isn't either. I hope you understand."

"Wow! You never told me how intense your experience with the Dream Glasses was."

Eric sat there shaking his head.

"You're an integral part of our team at Struthers and Sloan and I don't want you to go. But I guess I can see why you would want to give this a try. I'm happier knowing you'll be gone for a while instead of watching you move to Paris."

"Eric, that's sweet, but I have to give this a try! I'll be back. By the time I return, I'll know if baking's my future or if I have to find another career."

"I understand you need to go. I'll help you, but I'll miss you more than you know while you're away. And I'm gonna be here when you get back. I don't care if you're working for Struthers and Sloan or not, I want to know you will come home."

They left the bistro hand in hand. Liz turned to hug Eric.

"Thanks for being here for me. Your support means more than you might know."

Chapter V

The days at work passed quickly. The Dream Glasses project was in the hands of the phase two testing team. Liz was finalizing all her documentation. She found a nice couple to rent the condo, her passport and all the paperwork was ready. She was excited and glad to be leaving Struthers and Sloan. Friday would be her last day. She still hadn't figured out how she would say goodbye to Eric.

He stopped by her desk.

"I understand you're flying out Monday late afternoon and have things you still need to do, but it's important we spend as much time together as possible before you leave. Can we go to the Bistro for dinner, Friday night after your farewell party? We'll make plans for the weekend. I've taken Monday off to take you to the airport."

Liz's heart pounded.

"I'd like that! And thanks for offering to take me to the airport. That's so sweet of you. I planned to call a taxi. I'd rather be going with you."

Liz lay in bed Friday night with thoughts flying through her mind. There was no doubt she would miss her co-workers. She didn't know what would happen with the Dream Glasses, but she knew they unlocked her dreams. Dinner with Eric was sweet. She couldn't help wondering if there was something he wanted to say, but didn't. Or, did she hope he'd say something? They would have the weekend to spend together. With everything packed, the house was ready for her departure and for the tenants to arrive. She lay there thinking about how weird it is, knowing someone else will live in her home and how strange it'll be to not see Eric for six months. Her mind raced as she wondered what the future would hold for her. She drifted off to sleep.

The alarm clock awoke her with a start. The weekend passed in a blur. Eric took Liz to all her special places within the city and they dined together every day. Sunday evening Liz fell into bed exhausted. She was too tired to think. Before she knew it Monday morning arrived. She got up, dressed and walked around the apartment realizing it would be months before she was standing in these rooms again.

Liz had her bags by the door and was double-checking everything when Eric arrived.

"Hi. Are you ready?" he said.

Liz scanned the room one more time and spotted the Dream Glasses on her bookcase.

"Oh, my goodness. I can't leave these here."

She walked over and picked up the glasses.

"Eric, will you return these to the office for me?"

"No problem. We need to leave so you're not rushed at the airport," Eric said.

He picked up her bags and headed out.

Liz grabbed her purse, followed him outside then locked the door. She had many thoughts as she handed Eric the key.

"Thanks again for offering to take care of my place and make sure everything is okay with the tenants. I guess I'm ready to be off."

The drive to the airport seemed quiet and quick.

With her luggage checked, Eric walked Liz to the security checkpoint line. Taking her in his arms, he gave her a big hug and whispered in her ear.

"This is where I have to say goodbye. I understand you need to do this, but I also want you to understand I'm waiting for you here. Keep in touch and hurry home."

Liz returned Eric's hug, and gave him a kiss on the cheek.

"I'll let you know as soon as I land in Paris and arrive at Sabine's. Thanks a million for all you've done to make this trip possible. Don't worry, I'll be sharing this adventure with you."

Both were saying 'good bye' as Liz turned and entered the queue for security.

With her passport and flight documents validated, Liz turned and waved one more time to Eric before rounding the corner. Before long she was sitting at the gate waiting to board her fight. Once settled in her seat, Liz found her heart pounding and her thoughts flying in a dozen different directions. She wondered what Paris would be like; would she enjoy working in a bakery as much as she imagined; would it satisfy her; what did Eric mean, he's waiting; what about the language barrier? But, Eric won't be there!

The thoughts rolled on until she landed in O'Hare to change flights. She gathered her carry-on items and headed for the nearest reader board. Ah, she needed to get to Concourse C, Gate C20. On the way, she grabbed a pastry and coffee then headed to the departure gate.

Liz looked around the waiting area. The flight would be full. There were students who appeared to be off for holidays, several couples that looked ready to share a romantic adventure, and over in the corner appeared to be a group of businessmen.

Suddenly Liz wondered if she was crazy, traveling halfway around the world to help out a friend and test a dream. Then she realized this is a wonderful opportunity. She decided to just relax and enjoy the trip. Liz smiled, settled into her seat and waited for the boarding call.

Liz took her seat in Row 20A and glanced out the window as the plane took off. After the early snack and evening meal, the lights dimmed in the plane. She settled back and drifted off to sleep.

As the plane was descending on final approach to Charles de Gaulle, she woke up. She gathered her things and before she realized it was at Terminal 1, Gate V3. Natural light flooded the terminal, which seemed to heighten her feelings of excitement and expectation. She'd never seen an airport with such an open-air atmosphere. The escalators were all tangled together and enclosed in tubes, like a futuristic movie set. Liz used these escalators to get her luggage then move through customs. She was surprised at how calm and quiet such a busy airport could be.

Going through customs was a breeze. Liz gathered up her luggage and glanced around. Sabine was at the meeting point. After a big hug, she took one of Liz's bags and Sabine steered her toward another escalator to the parking garage. Liz realized the escalator system was just another part of her Paris experience.

With Liz's bags dropped in the back of the vehicle, she hopped in on the passenger side of Sabine's Volkswagen Polo and off they drove. Before Liz knew it Sabine was buzzing through the traffic and maneuvering the many roundabouts. The neighborhoods zipped past. She couldn't tell if it was because they were speeding down the streets or too many hours on a plane catching up with her, but she unable to focus.

Sabine said, "Few of the highlights of Paris are visible from this road, but we will spend time the next couple of days exploring the sights to get you comfortable here."

Liz said, "That sounds nice. I'm just enjoying being here."

As Sabine turned off the highway, Liz saw many of the streets, lined with tall white buildings. Balconies and small porches were home to various blooming plants or trees. Streets were clean; people were out and about. Couples were walking arm in arm. Children were tossing balls back and forth to one another. Besides the automobiles, there were many people on bicycles. There were even people out sweeping the sidewalks and gutters. The neighborhood felt alive and vibrant, but not hectic. Liz knew immediately, she would like Paris!

"How did Eric take your leaving?"

"Oh, he was great, especially when he learned this was not permanent; and he's looking after my condo while I'm gone. He says he's okay. I should call him when we get to your place to say I've arrived safely," Liz said.

"I'll park on the street. It'll be easier to get your luggage up to the flat. Then I'll move the car to the Faubourg Saint-Antoine Park House while you get settled. I'm so excited to have you here," said Sabine.

Liz was absorbing all the sounds and sights of the city as Sabine pulled into a parking place. Rue Antoine Vollon, a one-way street had parking on the same side as the buildings. The buildings had lovely architectural designs with black wrought iron balconies and door fronts. The street level, lined with businesses and some cafés sporting outdoor seating were filled with people. Upper levels provided housing, maintained with the same welcoming look seen on other streets. The flowers and green plants presented such a fresh appearance against the white buildings. Across the street was the Square Armand Trousseau Park.

Then Liz saw Blé Sucré. It was every bit as charming as the photo Sabine had shared. People filled the café tables and there was a steady stream of customers entering and leaving the shop.

"I thought we were going to your apartment? This is the bakery. I recognize it from the photo you shared with me. Wow, it sure looks busy."

Sabine hesitated.

"I guess I didn't tell you when my parents died, besides Blé Sucré I inherited the entire building. My parents lived in the top flat. I remodeled the kitchen and the baths and moved in allowing me to be closer to work. It's a great place. I hope you like it. Let's get your stuff upstairs."

Sabine helped unload the luggage then took Liz through the glass and iron arched doors and headed for the lift. Liz was breathless when Sabine opened the apartment door. She walked closer to the window and noticed the view out the living room window. Liz stood at the window and gazed on the Square Armand Trousseau Park below. From the street, one did not realize how developed the area was and how it buzzed with activity. Liz immediately fell in love with the park.

"Liz, make yourself at home. Check your bedroom. It's at the end of the hall. Put some of your things away or relax. I have to move the car. When I get back I thought I'd make us a light lunch. Sound okay to you?" asked Sabine.

"Yes, I could use a snack. After you come back we can relax together."

As Liz turned around, the full impact of the apartment hit her. Daylight flooded the room, making it bright and airy. Balconies flanked both sides of the building. The light and fresh air filled the room with life and freshness. Sabine's love of art showed everywhere. The white walls, the angles, the little nooks, her use of color for various accents made the place come alive.

"I love your place," Liz told Sabine.

Sabine smiled. "I'm glad. Your bath is right next to your room. My bedroom and bath are up in the loft. Make yourself at home. I'll return in a few minutes."

Liz found her room to be a lavender blue and white, with a small balcony. It appeared to double as an office area or small sitting room. The daybed hosted a huge pile of pillows and looked like a cozy place to snuggle with a good book. The mantle, which hung over the gas-fueled heater was home to a lovely vase and bottle collection in colors reminiscent of ocean glass. A large contemporary ocean scene was over the bed. Instantly Liz felt at home.

Liz glanced at her watch just as Sabine was coming down the hall. She knew it was too late to call Eric.

"Let's just leave my bags. I'll unpack later. I'd rather we catch up and enjoy each others' company."

"That sounds great. The bath is just down the hall. I hope you don't mind it's not private. It's used whenever people come over."

Sabine was already heading to the kitchen.

Liz followed her into a modern and convenient kitchen. Most of the cupboards and appliances were on one wall. There were rolling fabric panel style doors on the other wall which could be used to separate the kitchen from the dining area.

Sabine prepared the espresso, retrieved two plates, cups and saucers from the cupboard and coffee spoons from the drawer then headed toward the patio.

"Oh Liz, would you mind bringing the plate of cookies from the other cupboard?"

There they were. The same cookies Liz had enjoyed for weeks at work.

"Sabine, I can't believe you have these cookies here. This is a wonderful treat."

Sabine laughed.

"The cookies are Madeleines. The Blé Sucré is famous for these. Chef Nichol believes your first lesson should be your favorite item. I agree with him. The cookies will be your first cooking lesson. Before you review the business papers, I think it will be good for you to get a feel for the bakery and the staff. I hope you don't mind my deciding this for you. Please, sit down. Let's enjoy coffee and cookies."

For a couple of minutes they just sat looking at each other.

"You know, I can't believe I'm really in Paris."

"Me either. But I'm glad you're here.

Sabine looked at Liz.

"You know, I haven't heard you say anything about your parents. How are they?"

"Oh Sabine, mom's still with dad. I don't know why, but I've quit trying to figure it out. I talk with her and grandma often. I don't go back to Rosethorn any more frequently than I have to. Dad is paranoid everyone is after his money. Our relationship hasn't changed at all. Can we just not talk about this while I'm here?"

"I'm sorry. I can't imagine how difficult this must be for you. I won't bring it up again."

"Thanks! I want my time in Paris to be about the here and now. I don't want to deal with family issues – at least not while I'm here."

"I can understand that. Let's talk about other things."

"Okay."

They both sat quietly on the patio for a few minutes.

"Sabine, I'm sorry. I won't let my family, or should I say my dad ruin this time for us to be together. Let's start over."

"Okay," said Sabine.

They settled in and talked about the flight, Eric, what it felt like leaving San Francisco, the sights to see in Paris. The coffee, cookies, conversation and fresh air were all relaxing.

They sat there chatting and laughing for several hours. Liz relaxed and enjoyed the peaceful feeling.

Sabine said, "You look tired. We should call it a day. I'll be in the bakery tomorrow morning around 3 a.m. You can come down whenever you're ready. Everyone is looking forward to meeting you. Towels and everything you need should be in the bathroom. Help yourself to anything you find in the kitchen if you're hungry." She picked everything up and piled it onto the tray.

Liz could barely summon enough energy to get out of her chair. She smiled weakly.

"You're right. I should head to bed. If it's okay with you I won't decide about tomorrow right now. I'm just too tired. I'll wait until I wake up."

"Of course. You've had a long flight. How ever tomorrow works out will be just fine. Rest well."

Sabine was already heading to the kitchen.

After a quick stop in the bathroom, Liz headed to her room, dropped into bed and drifted off to sleep.

Chapter VI

The sun was shining in the balcony door when Liz awoke. She looked at the clock, surprised it was nine in the morning; she stretched and walked over to gaze out the window. She heard Paris had a plethora of little gardens and parks, dotting the city with greenery. The parks often intimate and sometimes a little quirky were jewels within the city. Liz couldn't believe her luck to be living across the street from such a place.

After dressing, the first thing Liz did was to call Eric.

"Hi. I hope it isn't an awkward time to call."

"Not at all. I've been waiting for your call. How was your trip?" said Eric.

"Uneventful. I slept most of the trip after changing planes in O'Hare. Total flight time was around 13 and half hours. You wouldn't believe the airport terminal here. It looked futuristic. The escalators branch and twist all over like the arms of some sea creature. Each of them is enclosed in these transparent tubes creating a strange atmosphere. Sabine was there to pick me up. I was surprised to find her flat is in the same building as the bakery. Oh. And there's this amazing park across the street. I have a wonderful view of the park from my bedroom."

"Whoa! I don't know if I can absorb all of this information so fast. It sounds like you've fallen under the Parisian spell. I'm not sure how I feel about this. We all miss you. I hope you have a wonderful trip. And good luck on the business mystery. I'm sure you'll figure it out."

Eric laughed.

Quietly Liz said, "I hope I'll be able to show this to you. I should get going so I can meet the staff. Let's talk again soon."

"Great. I'll call you over the weekend. Miss you," said Eric.

"Miss you too," said Liz.

Liz headed to the kitchen. She read the note Sabine left on the counter.

"Liz, we have coffee and breakfast things in the bakery. Come down whenever you are ready. Love, Sabine."

Liz realized she was smiling as she checked how she looked in the mirror one more time and thought it's now or never. Time to meet the staff. Nervously, she headed to the bakery.

The street bustled with activity on this sunny day. The café tables out front of the bakery offered limited seating. Some people sat alone as they enjoyed their café au lait and read the paper, but most people sat in groups, talking, laughing and enjoying their morning. The green umbrellas shaded them from the sun. The sound of children playing in the park added to Liz's perception this was an active and vibrant neighborhood. Before heading into the bakery she discovered the fancy metalwork of the Blé Sucré sign hanging just over the door. It provided an old world touch to the business. Fresh baked pastry fragrances wafted out the door. The bakery had been open for several hours and was still busy. Sabine saw her as soon as she entered.

"Liz. So glad to see you. Did you rest well last night? I want you to meet the staff. Camille, this is my friend Liz. Liz, Camille."

Sabine took Liz by the hand and led her into the kitchen.

"Liz, I'd like you to meet Chef Nichol and Alexandre. Guys, this is my friend Liz. I've told you about her. She'll be working with us for awhile."

"Liz, I'm so glad to meet you. Sabine has said so many kind things about you and shared how much you enjoyed the Madeleines. I'm looking forward to teaching you how to make these little treats," said Nichol.

"I'd like that. There is an abundance of delicious looking treats in the bakery cases. Do you make these every day?"

Nichol said, "Yes. We start every morning at 3 a.m. It's a creative performance. Everyone knows what needs to be done and we all have fun making it happen. By 7 a.m. we have the morning pastries in the cases, the chairs set up at the tables out front and are ready for our first customers. We keep right on baking until about 11 a.m. when we make sandwiches for lunch. In the afternoon, we bake breads. The after work crowd stops on their way home to have an espresso and buy bread or rolls to go with dinner, and we watch the cases empty. We use any free time to get things ready for the next morning. Late in the day, we receive our food deliveries. Then it's time to clean up, bring in the outside chairs and prep for tomorrow. I'll be glad to have extra help around here. The next couple of weeks are supposed to be hectic."

Puzzled, Liz shook her head for a minute.

"You're open every day from 7 a.m.–7:30 p.m. and the work day starts at 3 a.m.?"

Sabine said, "Almost. We're closed on Mondays, but those are the hours Tuesday through Saturday. Sunday we're open from 7 a.m.–1:30 p.m. Chef Nichol, I know you are looking forward to Liz being here, but you can't work her non-stop or she won't be able to stay for six months. You must spread out her work hours. And she has to have time to explore Paris and fall in love with our city. Liz, why don't you get a drink, grab a pastry and enjoy a seat out front and study how the lunch crowd works. Or you could head over to Le Square Armand Trousseau Park and observe the shop from there. I know you've had your eye on that park since you first arrived in the neighborhood. It would give you a chance to check it out."

Liz said, "Going to the park sounds great. Then I won't be taking a seat from a customer. I'll watch the crowd, enjoy the park and appreciate the neighborhood all at the same time. Thanks. I like your idea."

Liz pondered the scrumptious looking selections in the pastry case and settled upon a Paris-Brest and a large cup of café au lait. The Blé Sucré Paris-Brest is unique from everyone else's. Many places make theirs in the shape of a large donut. Here, they are similar to a cream puff, but shaped like a tire. The pastry is slender, larger around and almost looks braided. The pastry is then cut and filled with a vanilla cream filling topped with whipped cream piled high and a sprinkling of powdered sugar. She took her decadent breakfast and headed for the park.

After entering the gate she found a bench under one tree. It provided a good view of the bakery and still allowed her to enjoy the environment of the park. She settled down to enjoy her pastry and found it contained more than a simple cream filling. It was a praline of almonds and sugar added to the vanilla pastry cream to create a sweet, nutty filling. The flavor was delicious! From her seat, she had a perfect view of the Blé Sucré. The umbrellas were up, providing a shady spot for those who sat outside. There was seating for ten at the outdoor café tables. Many of the seats were full and a line snaked outside the entrance. Some of those exiting the bakery brought their lunch to the park and like Liz settled on a bench to enjoy their meal.

The sound of children playing at the park created a universal sound even though Liz couldn't understand anything they were saying. Looking around she realized benches surrounded the entire perimeter of the square. Tall trees and flowerpots dotted the dusty paths throughout the square, all leading to a carousel and various other amusements for kids. Moms were pushing strollers, many with balloons rising into the sky. A common sight was children with tall whipped ice cream cones. Everyone seemed so happy at the park. Liz imagined she had entered an enchanted garden, yet here she was in the middle of a busy commercial thoroughfare.

A group of children must have been released from school. They had on navy colored slacks or skirts, white shirts and each had on a backpack. They were talking and laughing as they hurried through the park.

Liz sat at the park absorbing the atmosphere while periodically glancing at the bakery. With the steady stream of customers coming in and out of the shop, she couldn't image how Sabine would lose money. Did she pay her staff too much? Was someone stealing from her? Had she miscalculated the cost of operation and didn't charge enough for her pastries? ...and how does the staff achieve working those immense hours? Liz couldn't imagine working those hours even a couple times a week.

Absorbed in her own thoughts, Liz didn't see Sabine until she sat down on the bench.

"You look like you're miles ways away. Is everything okay?" she said.

"Oh. Hi. I didn't see you heading this way. I love the atmosphere of this park. I guess my mind is running in a lot of different directions. I've been sitting here listening to the sounds of children playing; people chatting; I've been watching the bakery and the steady stream of customers. And I have to admit, I'm a little worried about the hours you're open and the expectations for staff – me included. Do you really expect people to work from 3 a.m. to 7 p.m.?"

Sabine said. "You imagined all the staff works those hours? No, Liz. Nichol and I are the only two who work anywhere near those hours. You met less than half the staff. We have another baker who alternates with Alexandre and another woman, Teagan who alternates with Camille. Josette arrives at 3 p.m. and works to closing. Don't worry. I wouldn't allow you to work the hours you were thinking about."

Liz sighed.

"I'm glad to hear that. I know I couldn't work those hours even if I wanted to try. Do you know how strange it is to sit somewhere and listen to people speaking and not be able to understand anything they're saying? Everyone in the bakery spoke English."

Sabine said, "I remember how strange English sounded when I traveled to the U.S. for college, but I had the advantage of knowing the language before I got there. Students here study English at a young age. Many French people speak multiple languages, but they may not let you know that fact. You should enjoy the neighborhood and rest today. Your flight was long and I remember it taking a few days to settle into the culture and time changes. Tonight we can have dinner at Le Rustres. It's simple, quiet, a neighborhood hangout and a favorite of mine."

"That sounds lovely. I think I'll walk the streets, then rest before dinner."

Due to the excitement of a new place and the travel fatigue taking control of her mind, Liz found it difficult to think in complete sentences.

"Great. I'll head back to the bakery and stop by the house for you around seven. See you then," said Sabine.

Sabine headed towards the bakery and Liz sat surveying the many children as they played on various amusements in the park. It was a beautiful sunny day, and she was so relaxed. It didn't take long for Liz to realize she all she wanted to do was go home and nap.

Chapter VII

Sabine arrived home just after seven. Rested and dressed, Liz was ready to go out for dinner.

"Wow. I'm surprised to see you're awake. I thought you might still be resting."

Liz said, "No. I realized I didn't have the energy to walk the neighborhood, so I came home and fell asleep. I'm refreshed now and starved."

Sabine grinned.

"I'm glad to hear it. Let's get going. Le Rustres is a small place."

Liz found Le Rustres to be a tiny restaurant with much atmosphere. The terrace had a few tables and from there one could see Le Square Trousseau.

"How charming. I didn't even see these tables from the park today, yet one could dine here and observe the activities."

The menu written on a blackboard, just as Blé Sucré does for their lunch menu, sat outside the door. Like the Blé Sucré, it was written in French and made little sense to Liz.

"Come on. You'll love this place. The food is simple French cuisine. The menu changes daily. Whatever the chef is in the mood to cook is what he serves. The whole neighborhood considers it one of the best places to eat. Tourists don't come here," said Sabine.

As they settled in their seats, the chef came to their table.

"Oh Chef Ivan, I want you to meet my friend Liz from the states. She'll be here for six months. Liz, this is Chef Ivan. He runs this amazing establishment," said Sabine.

Chef Ivan turned to Liz.

"It's a pleasure to meet a friend of Sabine's. I hope you enjoy your stay in Paris and I hope you'll be comfortable here at Le Rustres."

"Thank you. It's my pleasure to meet you and to dine here," said Liz.

Chef Ivan translated the menu options for the evening and left the women to choose their meal. Before they had made their decisions, he returned with Apricot Chambord Brie flanked by toasted baguettes and a bottle of white wine.

"If you ladies will allow me, I'll make your dinner selections for the evening."

Sabine looked at Liz, and shook her head in agreement.

"How can we refuse such an offer? The appetizer looks delicious. Thank you."

Liz and Sabine settled back and enjoyed a leisurely evening meal. Chef Ivan continued to surprise them with one plate of deliciousness after another.

"Do you ever cook at home with so many dining options available here?" said Liz.

Sabine laughed.

"Well, not as much as many Americans. But yes, I still cook at home. It's something I enjoy doing when I have the time. Otherwise, it's hard to dismiss the opportunity to enjoy such a meal and not have the work of cooking and cleaning up when you're tired after a full day at work. And one never knows who you'll run into when you're dining out."

"I guess I've never considered that. At home, when I eat out it's mostly to be social and I give little thought to the food. This is much more relaxing. I could get used to dining like this," said Liz.

"Have you considered when you want to start working in the bakery? I want us to work out a schedule you're comfortable with, and I want you to enjoy the charm of our city. I think you should take several days and get used to being in Paris. You can stop into the bakery, get to know the employees and get familiar with what we offer, but wait until next week to start work. I can introduce you around the neighborhood. If they don't think you're a tourist, they'll treat you differently. I guess I never gave you an opportunity to answer any of the questions," said Sabine.

Liz considered this before she replied.

"Everything is so new. I know my brain is working slower than normal. I look forward to meeting everyone in the bakery. I could use a few extended weekends to explore Paris, the rest of France and beyond while I'm here. Yes, please introduce me to the people I'll see daily."

"Great. The best time for us to go around the neighborhood meeting the shop owners is first thing in the morning, or shortly after lunch break. Which time is best for you? What do you say we head home for tonight? You look tired," said Sabine.

"Sounds good. This has been a wonderful evening. I am tired. Let's go after lunch. I'm still adjusting to the travel and the time change."

When Liz woke in the morning, Sabine had left for the bakery. She looked at the clock and found it was 9:30 a.m. There was a note on the kitchen table reminding her to help herself to breakfast or to come to the bakery. Sabine said she would be back after lunch break. Liz stood their studying the espresso machine. She wanted a café au lait, but wasn't sure she knew how to operate the fancy machine on the counter. Then she spotted Liz's French press. She fixed herself a café au lait and settled into a comfy spot on the balcony.

She daydreamed, seeing herself baking, Eric, living in Paris. In fact, she couldn't stay focused on anything for long. Without thinking, she watched the action on the street below and the park across the way.

Liz studied the chic Parisians, munching on pieces of their baguettes as they walked to the nearest velib shop. The velib shop presented options Liz had never considered. Being able to rent a bicycle here and then drop it off at another location in town might be one of the healthiest and cheapest ways for her to explore Paris. She made a mental note to talk with Sabine about this.

The girls coming out of Derbe Dedo appeared breathless and excited. They must be close friends. Liz wondered what their life was like that allowed them to take part in a midmorning dance class.

It was obvious the group entering Ben Azri were tourists. They were wearing blue jeans, baggy t-shirts and white tennis shoes. They stood out from everyone else on the street. Yikes! Liz knew she didn't want others to consider her a tourist. She did a quick mental check of the clothes she brought with her and remembered she left most of her jeans at home. Liz didn't want to stand out in a crowd. She'd heard too many stories of how the French people treated American tourists.

Suddenly Sabine was on the balcony with Liz.

"I can't get over the exuberance here. From early morning until late at night this neighborhood is buzzing with people doing different things. I even smell the bakery in the air. This is wonderful."

"The neighborhood is a special place. I was hoping you'd enjoy it. Are you ready to meet the local shopkeepers?" said Sabine.

"I am, but I'm nervous due to the language barrier."

Sabine laughed.

"You know, most of us speak English. Once you have a proper introduction, you'll have no problems. We stick to French, especially when we think tourists are around so we don't get bombarded with questions. You'll be fine. These are great people. You'll love them once you get to know them. And who knows, you may pick up some French."

Off they went. As they entered a shop, Sabine inquired in French for the owner and then told them she wanted to introduce her American friend, who would stay for six months and work in the bakery. The conversation switched to English for introductions and a short chat.

The shopkeeper at Kickers wasn't busy when Liz and Sabine entered the store. Introductions happened as in the other shops. Jeannine instantly connected with Liz and shared insights about the neighborhood.

"From the park, you can watch the local beggar and her baby. They sit right next to the bank entrance. She's claimed the same spot for four years now. The baby was a new born when they settled in the location. You'll find the child charming as he walks and talks with people on the street. People in the neighborhood make sure they're needs are met."

Liz said, "OK."

"Of course, our neighborhood is no exception when it comes to the ever-existing harmless crazy person. Every Parisian neighborhood has one. Ours has his foldable chair right next to Franprix. You will not miss him when you shop for groceries. You'll find him calling out to everyone as they pass. He has the best spot on the street and knows everyone and everything happening in the neighborhood. I'd be surprised if he wasn't already aware you're here. You'll only see him when the weather is good. Once it cools off, he'll pack up his chair and leave the space for someone else. You'll love it here. You'll discover the people in this neighborhood are the best. There's lots of variety in the neighborhood and in what's offered here.

There's entertainment, fabulous food, shopping, culture and the wonderful park. I'm glad we got to meet," Jeannine said.

Just then several customers entered the shop. Liz and Sabine said their goodbyes and continued on their way.

Sabine pointed to a building just down the block.

"Over there is the Bred Banque Populaire, our neighborhood bank. I suspect you'll do your banking there."

The little brown eyed, curly haired boy charmed Liz as he walked up and greeted each person as they passed by the bank. It was easy for Liz to understand why the neighborhood looked after the woman and her son.

They rounded the corner and the golden arches of McDonalds were on this Parisian street.

"Oh, please! Do the French actually eat at McDonalds?" said Liz.

"Some families take their children there. After living in the United States, I cannot understand what the fascination is when we have so many wonderful French restaurants to chose from," said Sabine.

"I should get back to the bakery for the late afternoon business. We could go to Le Bistrot du Peintre for dinner. It's quaint, cozy and another local favorite," said Sabine.

"I think it sounds wonderful. I'll stop back up to the flat and catch up on the news before dinner. See you later."

Liz headed back to Sabine's place and enjoyed a relaxing afternoon.

Sabine surprised Liz when she arrived home before 7:30 p.m.

"Are you ready for another taste of Paris?"

"Yes. I didn't realize how quickly the afternoon passed."

Le Bistrot du Peintre was in a perfect location, on the triangular corner of Ledru Rollin and rue de Charonne, with plenty of outside seating under the large awnings Liz was finding so common in the Paris neighborhood. Liz stepped inside and felt transported to another world. The hint of art nouveau greeting them as they approached the bistro continued inside with trompe l'oeil ceilings and a certain faded charm. Staff welcomed them and ushered them to a table providing a great view of the set-up bar; a rickety set of stairs the wait staff glided up and down; and a narrow intimate room off to one side. Tables were close, but this allowed them to see different plates as the waiters served those around them.

"I can't believe how many wonderful paintings are in this place." Liz said.

Sabine said, "du Peintre means 'the painter.' It's been here since the early 1900s and beloved by many local artists, celebrities and bobos, or enlightened elite as some say. And of course, the neighborhood locals love this place."

The bistro swiftly filled up with what appeared to be a mix of tourists and locals.

"It leaves me out of breath watching the waiters fly around this place. I can see what you meant when said du Peintre was popular. It makes sense to hear this place has been here since the 1900s. It seems I've stepped back in time. The room feels warm and romantic. I bet if these walls could talk they could share many a love story," said Liz.

Sabine looked at Liz.

"Are you okay? You appear to be miles away."

"Oh, I guess I was thinking about friends back home."

Before Liz had time to divulge any more of her thoughts, dinner and wine arrived at the table.

They enjoyed vegetable lasagna and a rib eye steak with chips.

"We must share their café gourmand. It is a sampling of their desserts with espresso. You'll find it a wonderful way to end the evening," said Sabine.

Liz said, "How can I question if dessert will be good after the dinner we finished? I'm game if you are."

The waiter appeared with two cups of espresso and a lovely tray of nectarine panna cotta, small orange tarts, lime macaroons and miniature Madeleines.

Liz eyed the dessert tray.

"Ah, Madeleines again. It reminds me they're the reason I'm here. I wanted to tell you I'm ready to look over the financial records of the business. I thought I'd start with the financials to see if anything obvious appears out of place. We don't have to count my first review as part of my work time. I figure there will be plenty of days in the bakery where all that's accomplished is training me. I want to feel like I'm doing something productive and learning something."

"If you're ready, I can get the records for you to review. I don't want you to feel like your time in Paris is all work and no play, so please don't push yourself too hard on this," said Sabine.

"Thanks. I appreciate your concern, but I should get started. If I finish up swiftly I'll have even more time to explore Paris. And once I have the mystery solved for you, I can focus more on baking. I'm struggling to figure out if being a baker is my future," said Liz.

Sabine laughed.

"Whoa. I hope you can figure that out at Blé Sucré. Speaking for both Nicole and myself, we'd be happy to teach you about baking and all that's involved in running a bakery. You're talking like the Liz I always knew. You wanted to get your work done way before it was due and then you'd breeze into class like it was effortless. I should have expected this. Tomorrow, it is."

Liz and Sabine finished their desserts and espressos then headed into the Paris night feeling satiated.

The next day, Liz woke to the morning sun streaming into her room. Her thoughts immediately turned to the bakery and her desire to start the research. She planned to review paperwork and then grab lunch at the bakery, say 'hi' to the staff and take a neighborhood walk.

Just as she said, Sabine had the last six months worth of financial papers on the kitchen table. Liz fixed herself a cup of café au lait, grabbed a croissant, and sat down to work. The fragrance of the smooth, rich drink filled Liz's head and she felt dizzy with delight as she dipped her croissant into the cup as she had watched others do in the bakery. Liz realized the café au lait in Paris was much richer than those served in the U.S. In Paris, the drink is made with espresso and steamed milk, unlike the brewed coffee and scalded milk she drank at home. She soaked the buttery croissant into her coffee brew, creating a breakfast treat fit for royalty. Liz loved the food and dining experiences in Paris. As she sat there, she realized she needed to get serious about learning the names of each pastry.

She took another bite and became engrossed in the paperwork. Completely absorbed in her work, she lost track of time. Realizing she was hungry, she glanced at her watch. It was already 1:30 p.m. She didn't even know if the bakery would still be serving lunch.

Liz stood, stretched and headed for the door. She was still thinking how busy the bakery always was and about the financial numbers she'd spent the morning reviewing.

The lunchtime crowd had thinned and there were seats at the outdoor tables. Bakery fragrances wafted out the door and reinforced how hungry she was.

Nichol was bringing out a tray of croissants as Liz was walking in the door.

"Well hello, Liz. Glad to see you again. Teagan, this is Liz. She's Sabine's friend from America and will work part-time with us for a few months. Liz, this is Teagan. She and Camille work alternate days in the bakery. They're both excellent with the customers. What can we get you today?"

"Hi, Teagan. Chef Nichol, I'll try your quiche today with one of those fresh croissants and a sparkling water. I'm starved. Can you tell?" said Liz.

Teagan's voice was jovial.

"You came to the right placed to eat because everything is delicious!"

Teagan handed Liz the plate with the quiche and croissant.

"Would you like raspberry jam to go with the croissant?"

"Oh yes, that sounds wonderful," said Liz.

"I'll bring the jam out with your water. Make yourself comfortable and enjoy lunch," said Teagan as she turned.

Liz selected an inside table in the back corner. From there she savored her lunch and could watch the flow of customers. She enjoyed watching the easy banter between customers and staff, and between the staff. The bakery emitted these wonderful feelings of warmth, friendliness and comfort. Liz found herself lost in the lively atmosphere of the environment, soaking in the fragrances of freshly baked pastries and the sounds of people interacting with one another. How could anything be wrong in a business where everyone seems to enjoy being here and working together? Even the customers love coming here. I guess I'll keep digging through paperwork. If there's something to find, I'll find it.

Nichol walked over to Liz's table, pulled out a chair, sat down and handed Liz a fresh Madeleine.

"I hope you are getting settled at Sabine's and enjoying your introduction to Paris."

"Oh, I am." said Liz.

"I hear you'll start in the bakery Monday morning. In honor of your first day I thought we'd begin by learning how to make Madeleines. We'll only be able to 'start' as the batter has to refrigerate overnight. You'll return the next day for the baking and frosting steps. I'm no different from other bakers in Paris. I believe my Madeleines are the best. You must try them from other bakeries and decide for yourself. I need to check the breads to see if they are baked. We need to be ready for the late crowd who stop on their way home. I'll see you on Monday."

Nichol turned and left before Liz responded. She noticed the staff was always busy. She took a bite of the Madeleine Chef Nichol had left for her. As the delicate orange flavor melted in her mouth she felt the excitement build within her. She was going to learn how to make these cookies.

Heading for the door, she saw Sabine and waved to her.

"I'll see you this evening. I thought I'd make dinner for us at home tonight."

Sabine nodded.

"Great. I'll see you later and I'll bring the bread."

She headed back to the kitchen to get another tray of fresh loaves.

Liz stopped at the market and picked up chicken breasts, fresh spinach, salad mixings and a bottle of white wine before heading home.

Sabine's kitchen was arranged and stocked with everything Liz could've imagined. While working in the kitchen, she realized how relaxed she felt and how much she had missed cooking. She prepared a chicken Florentine dish and set the table. Sabine walked in the door just as Liz was doing the final preparation steps for the meal.

"Wow. I thought we might have cheese, fruit, bread and wine. This is a feast!" said Sabine.

"If you cut the bread, I'll open the wine then we'll be ready to eat," said Liz.

As Sabine and Liz enjoyed their dinner, the conversation turned to the work schedule.

"Chef Nichol told me we'd start my training in the kitchen on Madeleines. I cannot believe I will learn to make these cookies, and I can't believe it takes two days to make them," said Liz.

"Yes, many discriminating desserts are time consuming. Often, they're made with few ingredients, mixed in specific ways to create a flavor or texture, which makes the pastry stand out from all others. Nichol is proud of his technique and recipe for Madeleines. I think you'll be surprised to find how much fun he has in the kitchen. What sort of progress did you make with the paperwork?"

Liz appeared unsatisfied and shook her head.

"None. From a paperwork perspective, everything I've looked at so far has the appearance of being okay. I need to complete reviewing the reports you've given me. I want to review these thoroughly before I go back further. It doesn't seem possible that anything is happening in the bakery. The staff I've met appear to be invested in the bakery and each other. I...I can't believe any of them are involved in something to harm the business, but I'll keep my eyes open when I'm there."

"I have to agree with you. I struggle to think any of the employees could be involved in sabotaging the business. Yet, something has to be going wrong. I'll offer whatever you want to help you sort this out," said Sabine.

She picked up her glass and finished her wine.

Sabine and Liz cleared the table and washed the dishes. Their conversation continued. "If you don't have plans tomorrow afternoon, I thought we might head over to the Gardens of Versailles. They're the formal palace gardens and I thought you might enjoy them," said Sabine.

"That sounds nice. I've heard they have bronze statues there. Yes, let's do that," said Liz.

Chapter VIII

Liz arrived at the bakery, early on Monday. Nichol greeted her as she walked in the door.

"Morning Liz!"

"Hi, Chef Nichol. You look like you're already busy. Are you sure I won't be in the way?" said Liz.

Nichol shook his head.

"No Liz. You'll find we have plenty to do here, but I think you'll enjoy it. There's an apron and hat on the table for you. You'll also find the recipe for the Madeleines. I'll let you look that over while I finish what I'm working on here."

As Liz put on her apron, she realized it looked just like what she saw with the Dream Glasses. Even the kitchen contained all the tools she'd seen. With her heart pounding she picked up the recipe and reviewed it. It was apparent either Nichol had provided this recipe to others or he had spent a lot of time getting it ready for her. The recipe was written to contain both metric and English standard measurements.

Liz thought it's obvious Chef Nichol is proud of his Madeleines. I hope to make him proud of my ability to bake. This will be a trial for me.

"Are you ready to start?" said Nichol.

Liz hesitated.

"You want me to take the recipe and just start?"

"Yes. If you have questions, I'll be right here. Ask."

Light-hearted banter and lots of laughter filled the morning. Liz found the recipe easy to follow. She mixed everything together and put the batter in the refrigerator along with the prepared cookie trays.

Between baking, questions and laughter, Liz learned a Croissant Buerre is nothing more than a butter croissant, and a Croissant Aux Chocolat is a chocolate croissant. But nothing Blé Sucré makes could be described as 'simply.' The croissants are far from regular. They're buttery with a delicate crunchy outside. The inside is soft and flaky. Not like American croissants.

The Kouign Aman is a butter cake. It is made from bread dough containing layers of butter and sugar folded in, similar to a puff pastry with fewer layers. The cake is baked in a low oven until the butter puffs up the dough, which creates the layering, and the sugar caramelizes the cake.

Liz, fascinated by the variety of the pastries, yet the simplicity of the processes, struggled to think by folding in butter and sugar you created layers in a cake; a cake made from bread dough. Yet the result was flaky, light and sweet. A real treat. She expected these delicacies much more difficult to make. The more Liz learned about baking, the more she wanted to learn.

"Liz, aren't you hungry? It's lunchtime. I think you should get something to eat and get ready to leave for today. Tomorrow we'll bake and frost the Madeleines," said Nichol.

"Lunchtime, already? I had so much fun this morning I didn't know it was so late. I guess I am hungry," said Liz.

"Like I always say, if it isn't fun, you shouldn't be doing it. Now get lunch and I'll see you tomorrow morning," said Nichol.

Liz laughed.

"I think I'll just have a salad with one of these amazing butter croissants and a latte. I'm heading over to the park for lunch and I'll see you tomorrow morning. Bye."

Liz found her favorite bench in the park. It gave her a view of the bakery, and the playground area. She could hear the sounds of squeals and laughter as the children played in the park. The location was so tranquil, it allowed Liz to rest and think about how amazing the day was. She relished working with Chef Nichol. She pondered finishing her Madeleines and wondered how he would like them.

Liz spent the rest of the afternoon with Sabine visiting the Gardens of Versailles. Then they headed to Le Rustres for dinner. "I'm glad you suggested we come here. It provided a relaxing end to the day," said Liz as they left the bistro.

The next morning Liz arrived ready to complete the Madeleines. She filled the prepared pans with batter, put them in the oven to bake and turned the Madeleines out to cool. Then she set up her trays with racks. After dipping the tops with a thin orange glaze, she lined each cookie up on a rack. She put the trays in a hot oven and watched for the bubbles to form on the edges of the cookies and pulled them from the oven so they could cool a second time. They looked just like Chef Nichol's.

Camille entered the kitchen and said, "Good. Chef Nichol's Madeleines are ready. The case is almost empty."

Nichol was right behind Camille and laughed his hearty laugh.

"Those aren't my Madeleines. They're Liz's. But they look as good as mine. I can't wait to try one. As soon as they cool, we'll bring them out front."

The days flew by with Liz working the mornings in the bakery, learning how to make new and exciting pastries and her afternoons reviewing financial documents. She started with current documents and was working backwards. She noticed the sales were consistent through all the reporting periods.

Sometimes the numbers would swing, but nothing too serious. When she inquired of Sabine about any of the swings, it was obvious there was a mid-week holiday when the bakery was closed, or there had been a special event. Things were looking fine until Liz compared the paperwork between Sabine's and her parents' operation of the business. The sales remained consistent between the ownership transition. She decided to ask Sabine about the food deliveries. Either she was using different vendors or prices increased. Cost of goods seemed out of sync with sales.

Evenings found Liz and Sabine in one of the local eateries or Liz cooked at home. Liz noticed Sabine had a close relationship with Nichol, but never saw them together except at work. In fact, Liz couldn't remember seeing Sabine out with anyone. They had become part of the local regulars who often frequented Le Rustres. They were going there again this evening.

Liz and Sabine had just sat down at a corner table when Chef Ivan came to the table with appetizers and a bottle of wine. Neither Liz nor Sabine bothered to ask about the menu, but instead trusted Chef Ivan with their dining needs. Both settled into their seats and enjoyed the atmosphere.

Liz said, "I love Le Rustres. It is 'so Paris.' Everyone is so comfortable here. It feels more like being at someone's home than being in a restaurant. Thanks for making sure I found these places."

"I'm glad you're enjoying your stay. Paris is like nowhere else. I'm prejudiced, growing up here and all, but there's a special magic in the neighborhoods. Sometimes I think the tourists see glimpses of it, but they don't get to embrace it. I'm glad you're experiencing the real Paris," said Sabine.

"Do you mind if we discuss work for awhile this evening?" said Liz.

"Not at all. Is everything okay in the bakery, or have you found something in all those papers you've been pouring over?"

Liz hesitated.

"The bakery is great. It's the paperwork I want to talk about. It appears you've not raised any of the prices since you took over the business, and sales have remained consistent. You've said yourself how great the sales are."

"They are. Business has been great and it keeps getting better. So…." replied Sabine.

"Well, it seems to be your cost of goods. Have you switched suppliers?" said Liz.

"No," said Sabine.

"Have you seen a boost in the cost of your supplies?"

"I don't think so. We can check with Phillipe to be sure," said Sabine.

"I haven't met Phillipe yet. What does he do at the bakery? And, are there other staff I don't know?" said Liz

"Oh, Phillipe. He's one of Nichol's assistants. He works on the days Alexandre is not there. I'm not sure why you haven't met him yet, but you'll love him when you do. You haven't met Sinclair either. You're gone before he gets there. He's our stock person. He works late in the day and takes care of our deliveries. He started with the bakery before my parents' accident," said Sabine.

"Hmmmm. I may have to shake up my schedule. I thought I knew everyone," said Liz.

"Let me know when you want to change your schedule so I can inform Nichol. He's getting used to you helping with the morning routines so we should give him notice so he can make different plans," said Sabine.

Liz said, "The sooner I change my schedule, the faster I can understand the ordering and receiving processes. Perhaps I'll be able to get the bottom of your problems quicker."

"Yes, I see. That'll be great. I'll talk with Nichol and make plans for you to switch your hours and let him know it's important for you to understand the complete process of running a bakery. I think he'll be excited as he feels you're a natural in the kitchen. You're not coming to the bakery in the morning, so we can discuss this over dinner tomorrow evening and work out the details," said Sabine.

"Wonderful."

The next time Liz arrived at the bakery it was just before 3 p.m. This gave her a chance to see both Camille and Josette. The afternoon crowd differed from the morning and lunch group who visited the bakery. People stopped for a leisurely cup of coffee with a pastry, or ran in to grab bread for either their evening or next day's meal at home. The one thing that remained the same was the high energy and the excitement between the customers and the staff. Sinclair arrived at the bakery about 4 p.m. and appeared surprised to find someone new in the kitchen.

"Sinclair, I'd like you to meet Liz. She's Sabine's friend from America. You've heard us talking about her helping in the mornings. Now she'll learn how the rest of the day runs. Liz, this is Sinclair. He handles our stocking issues and places the orders with the vendors," said Nichol.

Liz held out her hand.

"Glad to meet you, Sinclair."

Sinclair hesitated, looked down and then took Liz's hand.

"Nice to meet you, madam."

"Oh, please. Just call me Liz. Everyone does," said Liz.

"Ok, Liz. I've got things to do. See you later."

Sinclair turned away and was gone.

Nichol looked at Liz.

"I wouldn't be concerned about Sinclair if I were you. He keeps to himself and works alone."

"Ok."

Liz headed for the ovens.

"What's baking?"

"Oh, that's the fresh bread for our late customers. Because we bake all day long, when our customers arrive and pick up a warm loaf they say it's an extra special day for them," said Nichol.

How the baking never seemed to stop at Blé Sucré amazed Liz. She loved the atmosphere. Her first day of working the late shift, she and Phillipe met before he headed to his desk and then she assisted Nichol with whatever he asked her to do. She loaded the ovens with loaves of bread, carried steaming loaves to the display racks, astonished at how the customers just kept streaming through the front door. She and Josette exchanged brief greetings as she brought breads out from the back. About 5 p.m. the baking stopped, but the customers didn't stop coming in. The work in the kitchen changed from baking to cleanup and prepping for the morning.

Liz didn't see Sinclair again until they were finishing the clean-up tasks. He turned to Nichol.

"Are there any loaves of bread or pastries for me to take?"

"Yes, we have several loaves of bread left. We had a busy day. I think you'll find a few pastries to take with you," said Nichol.

Everyone said good evening and Nichol locked up the Blé Sucré.

That evening Liz and Sabine had dinner at home.

"So how did you find the late crew to work with?" said Sabine.

Liz said, "Much like the early crew. Everyone works well together and there's much laughter and gaiety even though everyone is working hard and meeting the customers' needs. I'm surprised by the quantity we bake and how so little is left at the day's end. Does Sinclair always take home the leftover bread?"

"Yes, Sinclair takes what's left at day's end, or whatever we don't want to save for the morning. He and his wife are involved with a homeless shelter near their house," said Sabine.

"Hmmm…," said Liz.

She immediately determined she would see how the receiving is handled the next time she worked.

"Are you OK tonight?" asked Sabine.

"Yes, I'm a little tired and perhaps a little homesick. Paris is great. I love being at the bakery, but I miss my friends. I guess you may have experienced similar feelings at college," said Liz.

Sabine said, "Ah, yes. I think I understand what you're saying. A new location offers many new and exciting happenings, yet a part of oneself never gives up feelings for their homeland."

"If you don't mind, I'll call it an early night and maybe read. See you tomorrow," said Liz.

She stood up and carried her dishes to the kitchen then headed to her room.

Sabine was cleaning up from dinner but couldn't calm the thoughts in her mind. She didn't know what she'd do if Liz decided to return to the states early. The business was all she had.

Liz headed to her room and was pondering how she'd spend her next few days off. She'd explored the neighborhood and was comfortable there; the business owners or those living in the area converted to English when she was present. They seemed eager for her to embrace their way of life. She found life in the neighborhood had an intense tempo. Yet everyone wanted to safeguard the traditional roots from the old and more rural days.

Parisians are serious about their culture, which was obvious even in this small neighborhood. Art was displayed almost everywhere one went, and it was common to enter a bistro during the afternoon or evening and find a group of writers reviewing someone's work and in serious conversation. People nod at these groups, but never venture to converse with anyone at the table. Their work was considered serious and valued by the community.

Liz liked the atmosphere of the neighborhood, yet recognized she was feeling restless and knew she should explore the city.

Liz knew it would take months to explore the city properly.

She'd heard Notre-Dame in the morning light was stunning. She decided she would go there the next day.

In the morning she headed to Notre-Dame. The cathedral loomed above the pedestrian Place du Parvis which she considered checking out later. She paid her entrance fee and purchased an English guidebook. Because of her interest in ancient history, it fascinated her to learn that the cathedral built on the site of a Roman temple took two centuries of toil by armies of medieval architects and craftsmen to complete. Since its completion, Notre-Dame witnessed many great events of French history. Many coronations and state funerals have been conducted here.

Desecrated during the revolutions, the building was rechristened, the Temple of Reason. During the nineteenth century the architect Viollet-le-Duc carried out and oversaw extensive renovations to the cathedral. The renovations included adding the spire and gargoyles.

Liz stood in the towering nave. She let the soft multicolor light, filtered by the stained glass windows fall on her as her thoughts soared. She felt a peace come over her and wished she could share this experience with Eric.

She found a bench in the quiet cathedral and just sat there absorbing the elegance around her. It was not until the crowds gathered she realized it was lunchtime and she was hungry.

She stepped out of Notre-Dame and found a street vendor. She purchased a bottle of cider and a crepe then headed down the street to the Square Jean XXIII. Notre-Dame and the park filled the city block, all part of the small island in the Le Seine River. Unlike the Le Square Armand Trousseau Park across from the bakery, Square Jean XXIII had large walking paths and small grassy areas surrounding the cultivated gardens. All the pathways were in line with one another, with a few park benches in the large open areas. There were no play structures for the children. The park was formal but spectacular. Everything seemed to be perfectly manicured. The Japanese cherry trees had bark that appeared to have copper bands surrounding the tree trunks. There were apple trees and linden trees; all pruned to perfect shapes just as one would expect in a formal French garden. Unlike Le Square Armand Trousseau Park few people settled in the benches, most just walked the paths. Liz wondered about this. The majority of the folks in the park were tourists, not locals. It didn't matter to her as she sat and enjoyed the quiet of the day.

Liz finished her cider and headed back to the Place de l'Hôtel de ville where she knew she could pick up the metro. She stopped to enjoy the charm of the Le Seine River and decided she should walk home. Someone should be able to give her directions.

The Place de l'Hôtel de ville was the building for City Hall. Liz was sure someone there could provide her directions for walking back to rue Antoine Vollon. She entered the building and looked around for a concierge. She thought what she saw was an information counter and approached the man sitting at the desk.

She knew her French was not good, but thought she'd give it a try.

"Excusez-moi, parlez-fois anglais?" said Liz.

The man stood and towered over Liz.

"Madam, I have been trained to do so."

Taken somewhat aback, Liz hesitated for a minute.

"Can you give me directions for walking back to rue Antoine Vollon."

"The metro is much quicker. Do you have the required fare?" he said.

"Oui, I have enough money, but I'd rather walk," said Liz.

The man scribbled out the route for Liz.

"Suit yourself. I would have taken the metro."

Liz walked out the building without noticing much about the structure. She was sure she'd just met the rudest person ever. No one in San Francisco treated tourists like that. Everyone warned Liz how arrogant the French can be. Now she'd experienced it first-hand.

The longer Liz walked, the more she thought about home and the things she missed from there. She also realized how much she loved being in the bakery.

Liz arrived home to find Sabine already preparing dinner.

"I thought we could spend a quiet evening in tonight. How did your outing go? Notre Dame is magnificent, isn't it?"

"Notre Dame is exceptional," said Liz.

"Is everything okay? You lack your normal excitement for architectural wonders?" said Sabine.

"Oh, Notre Dame was spectacular. Then I walked to the Square Jean XXIII. It was exquisite. I found it interesting how different the atmosphere was from Le Square Trousseau. One is a neighborhood park and the other more formal or an attraction for tourists. The gardens and flowerbeds were captivating, but I prefer hanging out at Le Square Trousseau. I walked home instead of taking the metro."

"Whoa. That's a lovely walk, but long," said Sabine.

Liz sat at the counter.

"Yes, it was a long walk, but I needed the time to clear my head. I'd always heard how arrogant and rude the French could be to tourists, yet in the neighborhood I feel welcomed by everyone. They treat me like I belong here," said Liz.

"Well you do belong here. Everyone in the neighborhood loves you," said Sabine.

"Today was my first real encounter with *the French attitude towards tourists* and it shook me up. It reminded me how much an outsider I am here. The experience left me conflicted. I feel so comfortable in the bakery and this neighborhood; I feel like I belong. But today I realized there are places where I don't feel like I belong. I found myself homesick," said Liz.

"I knew this day would come and I've dreaded it. Being away from one's homeland can be difficult. I'm thrilled you love being in the bakery and you feel at home here in the neighborhood. I'm sorry about today's encounter, but know this attitude is all too prevalent in Paris. Please don't let today determine if you'll stay in Paris. Help me figure out what is going on in the business and then no matter what you decide you'll always be welcome here."

Some days life seems so complicated and other days everything fits together. Maybe I feel unbalanced, but today I don't know where my thoughts are."

Sabine sat next to Liz and put her arm around her.

"Thanks Sabine. Let's have dinner and just enjoy the evening. I'll think about this later. Right now my focus is to resolve the mystery in the bakery. Next time I work, I plan to sit with Phillipe and talk about the ordering process," said Liz.

Chapter IX

Liz found Nichol putting the icing on a tray of éclairs.

She said, "Yum. Those look delicious. I hope you have nothing special for me today as I thought I'd work with Phillipe to understand the ordering process for the bakery."

Nichol shook his head.

"Ah paperwork. Yes, you must learn this too. But let me tell you, it's not as much fun as baking. You'll find Phillipe in the back office. I'm sure he'll be grateful for some help so he can get back in the kitchen."

Nichol returned to working on the éclairs and Liz headed to the back office where she found Phillipe.

"Hi. If you don't mind, I thought I'd work with you today. I still have no understanding of how you determine what supplies are needed."

Phillipe said, "You may find this boring, but it's a necessary part of the business. Chef Nichol says you've been doing amazing things in the kitchen. Pull up a chair. You can see what I do back here."

Liz pulled up her chair, as Phillipe handed her a list.

"These are the people I order from. The process isn't complex. Sinclair receives the stock, puts it away and lets me know what quantities we have on hand. Then he recommends how much to order. You know, it'll be good to have another set of eyes looking at this with me. Lately I've been feeling like I'm ordering more, but I'm not sure why," he said.

"First show me the process. Perhaps while we work through the steps something will become obvious to one or the other of us," said Liz.

As Phillipe and Liz identified the vendors and worked through the process of ordering supplies, Phillipe froze and looked at Liz.

"This is the first time I've realized just how much I'm ordering. Are we baking that much more? You've been working with Chef Nichol, has he said anything?"

"No, he's said nothing. How do you decide how much to order?" said Liz.

"Sinclair tells me what we need. Then I place the order. We need to talk with Sabine to see if she can shed any light on why we're requiring so many more supplies," said Phillipe.

Liz said, "I think that's a good idea. I'll go see if she can come here for a few minutes."

Liz found Sabine enjoying a cup of espresso and reading the paper.

"Sabine, Phillipe and I were wondering if we could chat with you about something we found when going over the orders?"

Sabine said, "Does this mean you've found the problem?"

Liz said, "I don't know if it's the problem, but something doesn't look right. Phillipe noticed an increase in the supplies Sinclair has requested him to buy. He asked me if we were baking more than before. You and I have already talked, and we know that sales have gone up a little, but not greatly."

"Okay, I think we need to talk. But why don't we wait until the shop is closed and then we can sit down with Chef Nichol after everyone else is gone? I don't want to alarm the others, yet I want to get to the bottom of this. In fact, why don't we all just go Le Rustres? We should be able to talk there. I'll tell Chef Nichol and you talk with Phillipe," said Sabine.

Chapter X

Sabine and Liz arrived at Le Rustres first and requested a table for four. It wasn't long before Nichol and Phillipe joined them. Chef Ivan rushed over to the table.

"Chef Nichol, I haven't seen you here in ages. I hope things are well for you."

"Yes, excellent. We would like to trust you with all the selections for the evening. But please bring a special wine. We'll be celebrating this evening," said Nichol.

Liz looked puzzled.

"I thought we'd be problem solving this evening. You consider that celebrating?"

Sabine smiled.

"Very well. I'll get a special wine. You can count on an evening you'll remember for a long time," said Chef Ivan.

He returned shortly with two bottles of wine.

"If you're celebrating, one bottle of wine is insufficient."

He uncorked the bottle and poured Chef Nichol a taste. Nichol turned the glass in his hands gently at first and then swirled the glass, closed his eyes, lifted it to his nose and then his lips. He let the wine sit in his mouth a moment before swallowing it.

"Mmm…This is wonderful. Thank you. We're in your accomplished hands tonight," said Nichol.

Chef Ivan left the table beaming.

Nichol looked around the table and cleared his throat.

"Now, down to celebrating! Sabine and I thought tonight would be a good time to share the news of our upcoming wedding with the two of you."

Sabine giggled. Liz just stared and then smiled.

"I had no idea. Congratulations."

Phillipe said, "I wondered when you two would get around to this."

Nichol said, "I know you and Liz thought we were going to talk about what's going on in the bakery, and we will. But before we start on that subject, we wanted to tell you since we are friends and work closely together, little should change in the bakery. This will be a fresh beginning for the two of us and we're thrilled. So tonight we mix business and pleasure."

"Good. We don't want to stop having fun in the bakery," said Phillipe.

"Right. Liz, I know you have been going over the books from the business. Have you seen anything unusual yet?" said Nichol

Liz said, "You sure do change subjects quickly. So far the only thing I've found is a steady increase in the cost of supplies. Sales have continued to go up a little, but the costs have escalated much more quickly. Phillipe and I were going over the order processing today and before we started, he noticed something. Phillipe, do you want to continue from here?"

"Thanks Liz. I was looking at past orders so I'd have a starting place with Liz today. It shocked me when I realized how much more we're ordering than just a few months ago. My first question to Liz was if she could tell me if we're baking more than we used to. She talked to Sabine, and here we are to discuss the situation," said Phillipe.

Nichol looked at Sabine.

"Phillipe, does Sinclair still determine how much we're supposed to order?"

"Bien sûr."

"And he stocks the shelves, right?" said Nichol.

"Bien sûr," replied Phillipe.

"When do we expect our next delivery?" said Nichol.

"Tomorrow afternoon," said Phillipe.

"Hmmm… Tomorrow afternoon you and Liz should handle all the bread making and prep work. Sabine will be in the café working. I'll assist Sinclair with the deliveries. That'll allow me to validate we're receiving the goods we've ordered and paid for. I know Sinclair signs for the orders and Liz has already looked at those documents. So either he is signing without counting or something else is happening. Let's start there. And by the way, the wedding announcement doesn't have to be a secret. Sharing our engagement and celebrating makes it less obvious to the staff about the four of us going to dinner. I say we do it again tomorrow evening to discuss what we find. Liz, I hope you enjoy an afternoon of full-time bakery work tomorrow," said Nichol.

"Happily," said Liz.

Focus for the rest of the evening was on the excellent cuisine and the upcoming marriage of Nichol and Sabine.

Sabine and Liz enjoyed the night air as they walked home.

"Did I miss something? I had no idea you and Nichol were serious about each other or even dating," said Liz.

In the streetlights Liz could see Sabine blush.

"Liz, Nichol has talked about this for a long time. He got my parents' permission before the accident. We agreed to wait and tell the others until I returned from the U.S. He knew I wanted your help on getting to the bottom of the issues in the bakery; he thought it was a good idea to have an outside person I trusted looking into things. By the way, he's enjoying working with you. He said you have a real knack for the kitchen."

"I'm happy for you. Thanks for some of the background information. I'm sure your folks would have been pleased about this. They knew Nichol. They'd worked with him; he was part of their lives and like family to them," said Liz.

They picked up the mail before heading upstairs.

"Liz, here's a letter for you," said Sabine.

"That's odd. There are only a few people who know where I am," said Liz.

She took the letter and opened it once they were in the apartment.

"Oh my gosh! It's from Eric. He's coming to Paris and says he'll be here shortly. But he doesn't provide a date or flight. He wants it to be a partial surprise. What is this about? Can I arrange my work days to be off while he's here?" said Liz.

"That's a silly question. Of course you can be out of the bakery while he's here. What a fun surprise for you. I know you're missing some of your friends and your life in the states. I'm glad he's coming," said Sabine.

"I think I'm going to call it a night. It sounds like we'll have a big day tomorrow and another late evening," said Liz.

She headed for her room.

"Night. See you in the morning," said Sabine.

Liz closed the door to her room. It had been an amazing day. Thinking about Eric traveling to Paris made her heart beat fast and her mind spin in many different directions.

She couldn't settle down due to her excitement about Eric. Finally, she'd be able to share Paris with him. She thought about Sabine and Nichol's engagement. How they managed to be so calm and businesslike with each other every day seemed unnatural. Was Sabine flirting with Eric when she was in the states? Liz questioned if she had allowed their past to color how she viewed Sabine's actions around Eric.

Chapter XI

The bakery was humming when Liz arrived. Sabine was working with Josette. She walked into the kitchen and looked around.

"Hey Liz. Great to see you. We'll finish all the bread for the after-work crowd," said Phillipe.

"Sounds good to me. I didn't hear Chef Nichol's laugh today when I walked in. It feels different."

"He'll be in later. He had a few errands to run," said Phillipe.

"Ok, let's get started."

As Liz and Phillipe continued working, the smell of fresh bread drifted through the kitchen and spilled over into the bakery area. The muffled sounds of Sinclair and Chef Nichol were heard through the delivery door. Liz and Phillipe looked at each other, then shrugged.

"I'm sure we'll hear about this later. Let's get the afternoon loaves out on the shelves," Phillipe said.

They each grabbed a tray and headed for the bread cases. Sabine raised her eyebrows in a puzzled look when they both entered the bakery at the same time.

Phillipe said, "Chef Nichol is back there with Sinclair, so we gave them some space. And because we were both baking, all the bread was ready to come out about the same time."

He smiled at Sabine and continued loading the shelves.

Sabine said, "Well, it's nice to have the shelves full of bread. The afternoon crowd will be here soon."

Phillipe and Liz re-entered the kitchen as Chef Nichol was questioning Sinclair.

"How could we end up with so much flour? There's not enough room on the shelf. You're the one who tells Phillipe how much to order, right?"

"Well, well yes. I do tell him how much we need to order. Perhaps he ordered more," said Sinclair.

Sinclair did not look at ease as Chef Nichol turned.

He said, "Phillipe, I need you to come over here right now. I have to figure out where to put all this flour. Why did you order so much?"

Phillipe looked at the flour stacked on the floor and saw there was no room on the shelf.

"I ordered what Sinclair asked me to order; just like I always do. How'd we end up with so much flour? We've never had more than what fits on the shelf before."

"Is it possible you misunderstood and simply ordered the wrong amount?" said Chef Nichol.

"I suppose I could've made a mistake, but I don't think so. Should we review the ordering history? We've been consistently ordering more supplies, and today's order was only a little larger than the last one. We've never had so much. It doesn't even fit on the shelves," said Phillipe.

"Yes, I want all three of us to go look over the order history. We need to figure this out so we can explain this to Sabine," said Chef Nichol.

Chapter XII

Later at Le Rustres, everyone was settled and Chef Ivan brought appetizers and wine to the table.

Nichol said, "Today was interesting. Sinclair admitted he's been telling Phillipe what to order, but had no explanation why we received more stock today than what would fit on the shelves. He also had no explanation how he could keep requesting more, yet it always fit on the shelves before. He seemed nervous when asked about this. I plan to continue working with him on the days we expect deliveries. Do any of you have ideas or suggestions?"

I feel bad I haven't recognized the increased order sizes before. Do we have any reason to question if the previous deliveries have been for the quantities we ordered? We should've been overflowing with flour long before today," said Phillipe.

"No. We've been using this vendor for a long time. Liz reviewed all the packing sheets, invoices and payments. After today's experience, I think we need to focus on our internal processes," said Sabine.

"With as much flour as we have, it'll be awhile before we order again. Next time Sinclair tells you how much to order, take down the information. Then before you order casually check the stock on hand to see if the quantities makes sense," said Sabine.

"I agree. I'll let you know when Sinclair asks me to order more," said Phillipe.

"Liz, how was working in the bakery today?" said Nichol

"It was great. I felt like I knew what I was supposed to do. Phillipe was there to make sure everything went fine. I felt like I belonged in the kitchen," said Liz.

Phillipe started laughing.

"Well, you do belong in a kitchen. You're a natural. It's fun working with you."

The next few days passed without event. When Liz wasn't working in the bakery she explored other nearby Paris neighborhoods. She loved her time in time in the bakery. It never felt like work. One day she had just pulled bread out of the oven, set it to cool before taking it out front, when she turned around and saw Eric standing in the doorway. He was just casually standing there, in his twill slacks and casual shirt observing Liz. His sun toned skin set off his blue eyes and sandy colored hair. His eyes lit up when Liz saw him.

"Oh, my gosh! You're here."

She ran to him and they hugged.

"You got my letter, didn't you?" said Eric.

The way he was smiling and his eyes were twinkling it was obvious he knew she received the letter.

"Yes. But this is such a surprise. I didn't know when you'd arrive," said Liz.

"Great. It worked then."

Sabine entered the kitchen and saw the two of them embracing.

"Liz, get out of here. Go enjoy yourself and show Eric around. It would be good if the four of us could hook up for a late dinner. Chef Ivan would enjoy meeting Eric."

Liz wasted no time taking off her apron and hat.

"Thanks. See you guys later."

She grabbed Eric's arm and headed out of the kitchen.

"Hold on. You don't want me to leave my luggage in the bakery, do you?" said Eric.

"No, we can drop your bags off at Sabine's flat and head back out, unless you're too tired after all the traveling," said Liz.

"Are you kidding? I want to catch up and spend time with you."

"Great. Follow me. We only have to go upstairs to drop off your bags. Then we can get something cool to drink and head over to Le Square Armand Trousseau. It's just across the street. If you get hungry we can come pick up something from the bakery or stop at one of the little cafés around here. It's a peaceful and wonderful getaway right out our front door. I love the park," said Liz.

They dropped off Eric's stuff and took a couple of drinks from the refrigerator and headed for the park.

Eric turned to Liz.

"You know, you look great. I stood in the doorway watching you for a couple of minutes. You were so comfortable in the kitchen. There was such a look of satisfaction on your face when you pulled the tray of bread out of the oven."

Liz said, "I do love being in the bakery."

She hesitated a minute.

"The problem is, I also realize I don't fit in Paris. No, wait. I'm accepted and everyone in the neighborhood treats me well. When I leave the neighborhood, I'm frequently reminded that I'm an outsider and this is not 'my place.' Whenever I experience such treatment, I'm immediately homesick. Here's my dilemma; I miss home and I love the bakery."

"Hmmm." Do you have a favorite place to sit in the park?" said Eric.

"I do have my favorites, but all the park benches offer great vantage points to watch the neighborhood activity. Whatever looks good to you will be a great place to sit," said Liz.

They headed to a nearby bench and sat down.

"It's so great to see you. I sure didn't mean to start our conversation with my dilemma. I've missed being able to chat with you about the things going through my head," said Liz.

"I've missed those chats as well. I've got a few things I want to share with you," said Eric.

"Do you think you could only bake in Paris?"

Liz paused.

"I guess I haven't thought about baking any place but here. Why?"

"I'm so glad you asked. I've been so excited to talk with you about this. Remember when I picked you up to take you to the airport, and you asked me to return the Dream Glasses?" said Eric.

"Yes."

"Well, I was so curious I took them home to test them. Your presentation suggested such great potential I wanted to see for myself. You only scratched the surface of what is possible for one to see with those glasses on. Are you ready to hear all this?" said Eric.

"I'd love to, but you just arrived. Are you sure you don't just want to relax today?"

"No. I want to talk with you about the Dream Glasses project. I'm glad you gave me the glasses. I would've never understood how they worked. You see the company dropped the project. The next testing group didn't see anything. Because of your credibility they extended the test when the second group saw nothing. It turns out less than 20% of the people who use the glasses see anything. They've been unable to determine why most people see nothing different and a few people see amazing things. And Struthers and Sloan couldn't risk promoting a product that worked for such a small percentage of the population."

"I can't believe it. When I had the glasses on, I was in a different world. It was real. I could see things, smell things and hear things. How could so many people see nothing?"

"No one's been able to figure that out."

"You said you saw things, but you haven't said what yet. Does anyone at the company know they worked for you too? Are you willing to share?"

I've been so excited to talk with you about this. But honestly, I needed to test the glasses out several times. I couldn't believe what I was seeing. They'd already moved on to a new project at work, so I didn't say anything. I didn't care what they thought. I knew what I was seeing. I think you already know I care a lot for you. It was tough for me when you decided you were coming to Paris. I dropped you off at the airport and just poured myself into work. I forgot I had the glasses in my car until one day when I was cleaning the interior. I brought them into the house and sat on the couch and tried them on. I couldn't believe what started to happen."

Liz said, "I don't know what you saw, but I know what you mean about not believing what you were seeing. That's what happened to me. And, because of my experience with the Dream Glasses, I had to come to Paris."

Liz noticed her breathing quicken. When she brushed her hair back behind her ear, she realized she was starting to sweat. She thought I hope Eric doesn't see how excited I am.

Eric said, "I know that now. In fact, what I saw is the reason I'm here."

"Hmmm. Tell me more. The glasses made you come to Paris also?" said Liz

"Yes, and no. I'm here because of what I saw when I had the glasses on, because of you, not Paris."

"Oh. Please continue."

Liz struggled to sit still and listen to the things Eric was saying. She fidgeted with her fingers as she listened. There were so many questions she wanted to ask, but didn't know where to start.

"You see, when I put the Dream Glasses on I stood on the landing outside the doorway of a building. The building's named 'The Madeleine' and you were on the other side of the open doorway. 'The Madeleine's' a bakery and the fragrances wafting out the door were unbelievable. You looked so happy to be there and so happy to see me. I had to talk with you about this, and see if your vision and this one fit together for us," said Eric.

"Wow! You do realize those cookies left on my desk are called Madeleines?" said Liz.

Eric paused for a minute.

"Either you or Sabine might've told me the name of the cookies, but I didn't remember it. Believe it or not I looked at business real estate and found the building I saw when I had the glasses on. It's a small, privately owned bakery, and it's for sale. Liz, I couldn't wait to tell you about it. I think it's something we should do together. Oh, darn! Here I'm spilling all these thoughts and I'm not even sure if you want to be a baker. And I haven't let you know how much I've missed you. I can't live with you away. I want you to come home and I want us to work on having a life together."

Liz's eyes start to tear. She threw her arms around Eric's neck and snuggled into his shoulder.

"Eric, I imagined us together so many times. I was afraid to share my feelings. Then I knew I didn't want to stay at Struthers & Sloan, but didn't know what I wanted to do."

"I didn't mean to confuse you this way. When I saw how you looked in the bakery, everything I wanted to share with you came rushing back. I know you'll need to think about some of this. Let's try talking about something else for a while. What time is dinner and why did everyone get so excited about the restaurant?"

Liz said, "Is this a dream? So many things I've wanted are coming together all at one time. You're worried about overwhelming me and I feel astonished, like I'm in the clouds."

"I hope this is a good thing. Now tell me about dinner tonight."

"Really? You want to talk about dinner right now?"

"Yes. We'll get back to everything else after I hear about dinner."

"Ok. I've wanted to share so many of my Paris experiences with you. Dining in Paris is such a rich experience, not just because the food is good. There are lots of good, no, great restaurants in Paris. The dining experience here is rarely just about the food. It's about whom you are with, it's about everything you've seen and done during the day. It's about how you got to that particular table, that particular evening. It's about your relationship with the chef and his staff. We're dining at Le Rustres tonight."

"Ah, yes. That's the name I heard at the bakery," said Eric.

"Sabine and I go there often. Chef Ivan is like a trusted friend. He sees us come in and assures us a good table. I haven't ever ordered anything there. He brings out food and wine then we enjoy a great meal; relax at the day's end; share stories or greetings with other patrons; and end the evening utterly relaxed. The restaurant is an old established favorite.

Once in a while a tourist comes in, but it's like a second home to many in the neighborhood."

"So does the chef bring out food because you don't speak French?" said Eric.

"No, silly! He's known for his excellent dishes and the regulars trust him. Oh, and in the neighborhood, as soon as Sabine introduced me as her American friend everyone spoke English. When I return home, I will have many fond memories of evenings spent in this neighborhood and at Le Rustres. This place has helped me fall in love with Paris. I'll be sad to say goodbye to these friends. I hope you enjoy this experience as much as I have."

"If I heard you correctly, you plan on coming home. I'm so glad!"

"Oh, I guess I did say that. Hmmm. Must've been a subconscious thought because I'm not sure I realized I'd decided. After your proposal, how could I resist?"

"Let's not worry about it and just enjoy this evening. I want to see Paris, or at least this neighborhood through your eyes."

"Great. I'm looking forward to sharing the area with you. I'll have some time off so we can discover more of Paris. It'll be more fun exploring with you. The others should be done with work at 7 p.m. and join us shortly after for dinner."

Arm in arm, Liz and Eric entered Le Rustres shortly after 7 p.m. Sabine and Nichol waved them over to a corner table. Phillipe was also there. Chef Ivan appeared with a plate of appetizers, a bottle of wine and a big smile. He held out his hand to Eric.

"I understand you're Liz's friend. Welcome to Le Rustres. May it become your home away from home."

Eric stood to shake Chef Ivan's hand.

"Thank you. I'm thrilled to be sharing some of Liz's Paris experiences."

Eric observed how relaxed everyone was and found himself introduced to many of the other diners. The evening was fun.

"This is a wonderful place. Do you come here often? Everyone seems to know you," he said.

Nichol said, "This is a neighborhood bistro. It's a gathering place for many who live around here. We come here after work with friends to unwind, share our stories and enjoy Chef Ivan's wonderful dishes. For many of us, we simply let him bring us what he wants. I've never been disappointed with a meal here. Hopefully, you'll want to return. Liz took to this place immediately."

Liz shook her head in agreement.

"I've eaten in several places in Paris and I love coming here. This place and Le Bistrot du Peintre are my favorites. The atmosphere is different between the two places, but both are vibrant and reflect the true quality of a Parisian neighborhood."

Sabine said, "We don't expect to see you in the bakery tomorrow Liz. Why don't we all meet up for dinner at Le Bistrot du Peintre tomorrow evening? Eric will have an opportunity to see both of your favorite places."

Liz said, "That's a wonderful idea. We'll stop by the bakery tomorrow to pick up lunch and then walk over to the Promenade Plantée. I've been reading about the area and wanted to go there. It'll be so much more fun sharing the experience with Eric."

"Great. Sounds like we have a plan for tomorrow," said Eric.

Chapter XIII

In the morning, Liz and Eric entered the bakery. Eric surveyed the pastry cases and turned toward Liz.

"How's anyone supposed to decide what to order?"

Liz looked around and laughed.

"It's hard. That's why people keep coming back, so they can try different things. The Blé Sucré started as a good neighborhood bakery, but the word got out and people travel to this neighborhood merely to stop here. Chef Nichol put this establishment on the map. You can order, or we can just ask Camille to pack up a nice lunch for us and be surprised when we stop to eat."

"I like your idea. Camille, will you pack a picnic lunch for two with what you think we'll enjoy?" said Eric.

"My pleasure. Hi Liz. I hope you and Eric enjoy your day," said Camille.

With lunch in hand, Liz and Eric headed to the Promenade Plantée.

"What makes this park so special?" said Eric.

"The park is a tree-lined walkway, built on top of an obsolete railway infrastructure in the neighborhood. Lots of parks are built on other abandoned railways, but this is the first constructed on an elevated viaduct. The parkway, famous for shops featuring various arts and high-end crafts, rises above the area. The Promendate Plantée was on my list of places to visit," said Liz.

"It should be fun. I'm glad we get to do this together. We'll be able to enjoy the shops, the beauty and a pleasant place to share lunch."

"Yes," said Liz.

They walked arms entwined to the Promendate Plantée, stopping to comment about the architecture or the gardens they passed. They found a quiet spot under a tree and sat down to enjoy the activity around them. They could see the Coulée Verte, a large green field, in front of them. They watched moms pushing strollers with balloons tied to the handlebars. Young boys ran around tossing balls back and forth. While they enjoyed lunch they talked more about Eric's experience with the Dream Glasses. He kept seeing visions of The Madeleine, and of Liz and himself expanding their relationship.

"I realize this might be abrupt, but I know I want to spend my life with you. I'd be thrilled if you would allow me to purchase a promise ring for you while in Paris. Then if you decide you want to pursue spending your life with me, I'll replace the ring with something more appropriate," said Eric.

"Oh Eric. It may seem out of character for me, but my answer is yes. Yes! How could I not say yes. All I think about is you when I'm not baking? However, I want to share the European idea of rings with you," said Liz.

"Is it so different than ours?"

Liz said, "Yes. The stones in wedding rings are not so large, and the Parisians don't look to replace or upgrade their bands after several years. The original ring is a cherished item. If we purchase ours in Paris, it'll have double meaning for me."

"I like the idea. Could you explain the double meaning?"

"Sure. For me coming to Paris was an opportunity to explore a dream and find out if it was real. Leaving you in the states was difficult for me. I knew I was developing strong feelings for you, but didn't know how you felt. Now you're here in

Paris sharing the truth about your feelings. In Paris I've learned my dream is real. I love baking and know I want to start a bakery. What could be better than having two dreams fulfilled in Paris and having our wedding rings symbolize all that?" said Liz.

"Wow. Sometimes you can be a complicated woman. It'll take me years to understand you. Yes. Let's find our rings in Paris."

They finished lunch watching others enjoy the park.

"Shall we see if there are jewelry stores around here?" said Eric.

"That should be fun."

After a busy afternoon of exploring shops, Liz and Eric met Sabine, Nichol and Phillipe at Le Bistrot du Peintre as agreed.

"This is one of your regular hang-outs? It's so different from Le Rustres. I love the art displayed everywhere," said Eric.

"It's a splendid place. Different from last night. Both places are great fun," said Liz.

As they approached the table and joined the group, it was obvious there was much tension and excitement in the air.

Phillipe said, "Liz, I'm glad you're here. We have so much to talk about."

"I hope it's good news," said Liz.

"Today the strangest thing happened at the bakery. Sinclair requested more flour. When I suggested we go double check our on hand supplies he broke down crying. He said, 'you don't understand! I need to give supplies to my wife for the homeless shelter. Donations have dropped off. We don't enough food to supply all the people who come to eat.'"

"What was he trying to tell you?"

"I calmed him down and told him I needed to understand how we could keep ordering so much and yet it always fit on the shelves. At first he hesitated, but I persisted, insisting an answer was necessary. He explained he always parks his van in the back. He would sign for the supplies and the vendor would leave. Then he would put part of the order in his van and load the rest on the shelves. If the shelves were full and there was additional stock, he'd put that in his van also. He continued pleading with me about how short the shelter was on food. I told him I couldn't order flour today, but we were all meeting for dinner and would discuss this tonight. One of us would get back to him tomorrow."

"Wow. I never imagined," said Liz.

Sabine turned to Liz.

"What can I do? I've always had a soft spot for the homeless shelter. So I let Sinclair take all the bread, and other leftovers when we close."

Liz glanced around the table and paused for a minute.

"Sabine, I don't know all the legalities in France, or the tax rules. First you must decide how you feel about this. Do you trust Sinclair? Have you had other problems with him and do you think he's only taking flour for the shelter? Do you want to support the shelter? You must answer those questions before you even worry about the tax and legal questions."

Nichol looked at Liz.

"You look different tonight. So, not being in the bakery improves your looks?"

Liz blushed and looked at Eric.

"No."

Eric said, "It was an extraordinary day for us."

"Tell us more," said Sabine.

Almost on queue, everyone at the table leaned forward.

"Tonight may not be the best time for this conversation. Your day was so hectic," said Liz.

Phillipe said, "That's a good reason for you to tell us about your day. Out with it, now!"

Eric laughed, looked around the table and let his eyes rest on Liz.

"I presented a double offer to Liz today – and she said 'yes' to both. I asked her to marry me and to open a bakery together called, 'The Madeleine.' We hope you won't mind our naming the bakery after your cookies?"

Nichol said, "First, they are not 'my' cookies and I would be flattered if you named a bakery in honor of me. Liz will be an exceptional baker. I hope she'll let me share some of my recipes with her. You two make an awesome couple. It's obvious by how she perked up when you arrived, how important you are to her. You don't plan on stealing her away so soon, do you?"

"Well, I… you see we haven't talked about the when. I'm still just enjoying knowing this is all going to come together. I was thinking the sooner the better. But those are just my feelings."

"Eric's right. We haven't talked about how or when all this comes together. See, I told you tonight's too soon to talk about all this. Here you guys have all these questions; we have no answers for you yet. I'm walking on air," said Liz

Liz paused. Everyone was quiet, waiting for her to continue.

"I suspect in a few days, after we've explored Paris together and talked more, we'll be prepared to share all the details with you."

Sabine and Liz enjoyed a leisurely walk back to the flat. Eric remained at Le Bistrot du Peintre with Nichol and Phillipe.

"I'm happy for you. I must admit you surprised me. Eric seems like a great guy. Do you want to combine our weddings?" said Sabine.

"I surprised you? You surprised us with your wedding news. I didn't know you and Nichol were any more than working buddies."

Sabine laughed, "That's fair. We could have a double wedding."

"As romantic as a Paris wedding sounds, I suspect our choice will be a wedding in the states, then both of our families can be part of the celebration. I'll mention it to Eric while we are out and about the next couple of days. I'm unaware of his travel plans or how long he is planning on staying in Paris. Silly me," said Liz.

"Well, it would be fun to share our weddings, but I understand your desire to have family present. Nichol and I have no family here. Tell me what you and Eric decide after talking about it."

"Thanks, I will. I can understand your sadness of not having your parents at your wedding. On a different note, how will you handle Sinclair?" said Liz.

"I want to sleep on it before I decide. Remember, you're the reason we identified where the profits were going. Don't worry about it! I want you and Eric to enjoy your days exploring Paris and the surrounding areas. Have fun and enjoy this time to make plans for your future. Sleep well."

Sabine headed for her room and Liz just looked around the kitchen. She realized how much she enjoyed herself in Paris. It surprised her how much she'd changed and what she'd learned about herself in such a short time. She couldn't believe the reality that she was studying to be a baker under one of Paris' best and her future with Eric left her floating on air. She drifted down the hallway and fell into bed.

Chapter XIV

Liz got up around 10 a.m. and found Eric in the living room browsing on his laptop.

"Hi girl. Let's go look for our rings. Are you ready or do you have other plans for us?"

"Nope. No plans for today. Did you get enough sleep? It seems like you've been going non-stop since you arrived. I took a few days getting adjusted to the time change," said Liz.

"Maybe seeing you again has energized me. I'm fine. Trust me. Do we eat here or pick up something at the bakery, or someplace else?"

"Let's get breakfast at the bakery; we can leave from there."

While Liz and Eric were walking she told him of all the French wedding traditions Sabine talked about. Eric stopped and looked at her.

"Are you saying you want to be married in France?"

"Whoa. No, I don't want to get married in France. But I'd like to take some of the traditions home and integrate them into our marriage plans. I love how the basic concept is not just the wedding for the couple, but the actual joining of two families. It's a life event extending beyond the two people getting married. I love the focus is on the relationship and not the big production we've turned weddings into in our culture."

Liz had been talking faster and faster as she got more excited thinking about this and the reality of her upcoming marriage to Eric.

"This sounds important to you and I'd like to understand more of the French tradition so we can figure out what parts we can consolidate into our wedding. Liz I'm amazed by you. Sometimes you think so deeply about things and see stuff others seem to miss. I love this about you."

They continued walking and talking. Eric liked the idea the two of them would pick out the rings together. He wasn't so sure about holding on to her engagement ring until after telling their parents because he felt proud to think she'd wear his ring and would become his wife. Yet the more she talked about the benefits of this tradition and saw she yearned for their wedding to be a family-oriented affair and not a production for someone else's financial gain, he could see the advantages.

"For the French, the original meaning of the ceremony isn't overshadowed by the efforts to impress, outshine or dazzle others. The wedding day is designed for good old-fashioned enjoyment. A French wedding is about the coming together of two people by extension, the coming together of two families. The party to follow celebrates those unions and is not dictated by cultural whims. That's what I want for us," said Liz.

"It sure sounds less formal, and much more meaningful than some of the recent weddings I've attended. What about the rings?" said Eric.

"Hmmm. I'm not sure. We have to shop together. I want us to have simple matching bands. Whatever we decide on an engagement ring, I hope you'll understand I won't be wearing it every day."

"I don't understand your feelings about the engagement ring. Why wouldn't you want to wear it?" said Eric.

"Oh, I didn't say I wouldn't want to wear it. When I'm baking, my hands are always in things. An engagement ring will get dirty. I hope you understand and if it bothers you, we don't have to purchase one. I'm flexible about an engagement ring," said Liz.

"Let's see what's available and what we like. I suspect it'll become more obvious when we see what the options are."

After a day of shopping, laughing and exploring various jewelry shops, they found the bands they wanted to represent the rest of their lives.

Eric was insistent about an engagement ring, and Liz relented when they found a blue sapphire solitaire with small diamonds on either side going down the band. Eric was eager to return to the states to talk with his parents. They planned to talk with Liz's parents when she returned from France. The wedding would be at Eric's family vineyard. They planned, laughed and giggled throughout the day. Eric would check out the building for sale and make arrangements for Liz's return and her new career. The two of them enjoyed several days wandering around Paris, but their minds were already on the future.

Chapter XV

Under protest, Eric agreed to allow Sabine and Liz to drive him to the airport.

"Really, I'll call a cab. That's how I arrived. Then I won't be interrupting so many schedules. I'll be fine."

Sabine said, "No! You're not doing that. I suspect it'll be hard enough for Liz to focus on the bakery once you leave. We'll take you. Liz will see you off and say goodbye at the airport."

"Sabine's right. I'm not saying goodbye to you and watching you pull away in a cab," said Liz.

"All right, already. I get the message. It's hard enough to change one woman's mind, but changing two is impossible."

Sabine was up early in the morning. Breakfast was on the table waiting for them.

"Let's get going. We don't want to arrive late at Roissy."

"Wait! My flight is out of the Charles de Gaulle Airport. Are you sure it wouldn't be better for me to catch a cab?" said Eric.

"Silly. That's where we're going. We locals call the airport Roissy, or Roissy Airport," said Sabine.

Liz and Eric sat quietly in the back seat as Sabine pointed out highlights and points of interest while driving to the airport.

Sabine parked the car and turned to Liz.

"I'll wait here. You can go as far as the third floor with Eric."

She turned to Eric.

"I'm glad you made the trip to Paris. I'm thrilled you and Liz are getting married and will start a bakery. Those two events will ensure we meet regularly. Nichol and I look forward to connecting with again soon."

"Thanks for your hospitality. I'm glad I got to know both you and Nichol better. I hope you'll both be able to attend our wedding. ...And thanks for helping Liz identify how important baking is to her. See you soon," said Eric.

He hopped out of the car and grabbed his bag from the trunk.

Liz stepped out of the car. As the two of them headed to Terminal 1 Eric turned and looked at her.

"You look like you're a million miles away. Is everything ok?"

"Oh, yes, sort of. I was thinking about how differently I felt when I arrived at this terminal compared to right now. I'm glad you had so much time to spend in Paris with me. But, I'm sad you're leaving and I'm not going with you."

Eric saw the tears forming in her eyes.

He said, "It's only a short while, and you've so much to learn from Nichol. With his approval to name the place, 'The Madeleine' I'm sure you want a few more French recipes. I'll get things wrapped up with the building and talk with my folks about hosting the wedding at the vineyard. They'll be thrilled about the wedding. Then you'll be home. It will be full speed ahead on completing our wedding plans. Liz, I love you so much and I'm so excited about our future."

They walked into Terminal 1 hand in hand and headed for the escalators to Level 3. Eric's check-in was smooth. The attendant instructed him to go to Level 4. He hugged Liz just before he stepped onto the escalator. She stood there watching as he rose to the next level. Just before he was beyond her sight, he looked back, waved, then blew Liz a kiss. She returned the gesture and watched him move out of sight. Her heart was torn, but she managed to control the tears. She was excited about her future and knew Eric needed to be back in the states to prepare things, yet she was sad to see him leave after committing to their future.

Liz slowly walked back to Sabine's car. She opened the door, plopped down in the seat and stared out the window. Sabine looked at her.

"You look how I felt when I got on my flight to come to America to talk with you. I had no idea what was ahead of me, how I was going to handle seeing you or what would happen. Come on, girl. You are in a totally different place than I was. Yes, you just said good-bye to Eric, but only for a little while. Nichol and Eric seem to get along well. I don't want to lose touch with you again. Our friendship is too important to me. You'll only be here for a little while, then I'll be bringing you to the airport and you'll be the one on the plane."

"I guess you're right. I have so much to learn. And so little time left in Paris. I'm sorry. Saying good-bye is so hard for me. Have we resolved the bakery problems? Are you comfortable with what we've found?" said Liz.

"Liz, you helped us get to the bottom of the problems. Nichol and I have talked about this. We both think the Homeless Shelter provides a viable service within the neighborhood. We've decided we want to support it on some level. Yet neither of us is comfortable with how Sinclair took it upon himself to use our accounts to give food to the shelter. It was difficult, but I let Sinclair go. I don't think I could ever trust him again. Nichol and I want you to spend as much time in the bakery as you would like, learning what interests you."

"I can imagine it was hard to let Sinclair go. I'm sure you and Nichol will figure out a way to support the shelter if you want to. And, you're right. I'm eager to focus on learning the basics and things I must know to set up a bakery. My goal is to be successful, like Blé Sucré. I want you and Nichol to be proud of helping me get started in the business," said Liz.

"Great. We're looking forward to helping you."

During the drive back to the neighborhood Liz realized she was looking at everything with new eyes. She saw many sights, which would always hold good memories for her. Liz also realized Paris, or at least the 12th arrondissement would be like a second home to her. Once outside the neighborhood people were only too willing to remind her she was an outsider. She was so grateful for the memories in the neighborhood and how many people treated her like she was family and belonged there. It would be sad saying goodbye to all these new friends.

"I think you should just take the afternoon and relax. We can meet up at Le Rustres for dinner. Nichol might join us," said Sabine.

"Sounds like a good plan, except I may stop in the bakery to get a sandwich or something first."

Liz picked up a chive tomato sandwich and a soda from the bakery then headed back to Sabine's flat. She spent the afternoon contemplating the last couple of weeks and her future. She realized she only had three weeks left in Paris herself. She got serious about making a list of things she hoped to learn from Nichol while she was still here. As eager as she was to be in the next phase of her life, she couldn't understand how she would say goodbye to her new friends in Paris.

Then she reflected on how each of them changed her life and how much she had experienced. She smiled when she realized how amazing the adventures of Paris had been. And she knew much of what she learned would help make 'The Madeleine' a success.

It was just Liz and Sabine for dinner. As they were enjoying dinner, Sabine leaned across the table.

"I'm kinda glad Nichol couldn't make it tonight. We don't have many evenings left together, and I thought girl talk might be nice," said Sabine.

"It is nice, just the two of us. It's kinda like our first evening here, only now I feel at home."

"Yes, it is nice. Thanks Liz, for leaving your home and coming here to help me solve the problem with Blé Sucré. But more than that, thank you for giving our friendship another chance. I know I've said it before, but you're a special friend."

"I wasn't sure how I'd feel about being here, but I'm so glad I came. Now we each have better memories of our time together than how we ended back in college."

"That's for sure!"

"Thank you for being my friend. It's been a pleasure to watch you and Nichol working together. I'm grateful for how you opened your home and shared your life with me. As Americans, we romanticize everything about Paris. You helped me figure out if being a baker was just a fantasy or a passion. And Nichol has helped me learn so many of the inside ropes of running a first class bakery. I've learned a lot about friendship, forgiveness and baking all in the beautiful city of Paris," said Liz.

Chapter XVI

When Liz arrived at the bakery in the morning Nichol was singing and already taking pastries out of the oven.

"Welcome back. I wasn't sure if you'd return to work or not after Eric headed back to the states. Sabine reminded me you leave in three weeks. We have some serious work ahead of us."

Liz laughed.

"Yes, we have some serious work. I want to know everything you think is important."

"Let's go in the office and talk about what type of bakery you want to run. I'll make suggestions, but you must tell me what things you want to learn as well. I'll be happy to share my recipes and secrets with you. But, when you learn something new and exceptional, you must remember me and share the recipe," said Nichol.

When they left the office, Liz had a long list. Nichol thought she needed to have several bread recipes, the standard croissant recipe, the basic cake recipe and cream fillings for cakes.

Liz's additions to the list were some of Blé Sucré famous sweet treats. She must learn how to make the Paris-Brest. It was the first sweet she ate from the bakery. Then she added éclair, torte and soufflé chocolat mandarin to her list.

Chef Nichol laughed.

"You need to add some of the fancier desserts to your menu if you want the reputation for having French bakery items," he said.

"What do you mean?" said Liz.

"If you learn to make brioche and flan, you'll also be able to make crème brulee brioche. Likewise, if you learn to make fondant au chocolat you can decorate exquisite cakes. If you make light cakes with delicate flavored cream fillings and decorate them, you'll set yourself apart from other bakers. The fondant can also be a base in candy making. See how the different bases work together creating delicious treats?"

"Oh. I see how this can work. Can I learn all this before I leave?" asked Liz.

"Of course. I've watched what a quick learner you are. Remember, you have a natural talent for identifying flavors to complement one another. Let's get started!"

The days flew by with Liz learning new baking methods and more recipes than she imagined would be possible. She spent her evenings at Le Rustres or Le Bistrot du Peintre.

One evening while dining there with Sabine and Nichol, Liz realized there wouldn't be many more evenings like this. This time was coming to an end. She became reticent as she looked around the restaurant and at Sabine and Nichol.

"As you get more comfortable with the basics you'll find you can add little things to the recipes, making new desserts. You'll discover which ones your customers favor and then can expand your menu from there. But remember the most important thing I've taught you in my kitchen," said Nichol.

"Yes," replied Liz.

Both Nichol and Liz said, "If it isn't fun, don't do it!"

Nichol reached down to the floor and handed Liz three boxes, in varying sizes and told her to open them, the smallest first.

The first box was a wooden recipe box, containing all the recipes Liz and Nichol had been working on since she arrived in Paris.

"I've added a few more you haven't tried yet, but expect before long you'll also be making them. Sabine told me of your plan to make your bakery gluten-free and you've been converting the Madeleine recipe. As you convert and refine the recipes, I hope you'll share them with me," said Nichol.

"Of course. How can I thank you?" said Liz.

"Just keep opening the boxes."

Liz looked at Sabine who smiled.

"He's the chef. You must do what he says."

The next box was a white apron with 'Le Madeleine' embroidered on it.

"Oh, this makes my bakery feel real," said Liz.

Nichol said, "I should hope so after all the work we've put in during these six months. You still have one box to open yet."

Liz opened the last box. Tears welled up in her eyes.

"I thought these hats were reserved for distinguished chefs."

Sabine hugged Liz.

Nichol said, "You're on your way to being a distinguished chef. I don't let just anyone study under me. You've earned your own toque blanche. We commonly refer to them as the toque, but it means white hat. Please accept this gift from me and wear it proudly."

Liz looked around the table. She had tears in her eyes and was afraid to speak. She swallowed hard and said, "Thank you. Thank you so much."

Nichol ordered another bottle of wine.

"We need to celebrate tonight. You and Sabine are going shopping tomorrow and then you'll head back to America."

The three finished the wine and went outside. Nichol said good night. Liz and Sabine headed home.

Liz said, "What's Nichol talking about, us shopping tomorrow?"

"I can't pay you for all the hours you worked the last couple of weeks, so I'm taking you shopping. That way you can take a little Paris home with you. You've become a new woman while here. You need new clothes for the new you. See you in the morning."

Sabine laughed as she left the room.

Liz sat there and shook her head. She thought about how unreal and how wonderful the day had been. She realized she was tired but wondered if she'd be able to sleep. She knew she needed to go to bed.

Once in her room, Liz realized tomorrow would be her last full day in Paris. Memories of all the places she visited, all the people she met and all the new foods she was introduced to were her thoughts as she drifted off to sleep.

Liz and Sabine left early in the morning. They shopped and shopped. Liz loved the billowing blouses and tight slacks Sabine picked out. And a shopping trip for women wouldn't be complete without several pairs of shoes and a new bag. While enjoying lunch they talked about how they'd keep in touch and discussed future opportunities to meet up while traveling. They were still laughing when they arrived back at Sabine's home.

"Let me help you get this all packed so you can relax this evening. Tomorrow will come quickly enough," said Sabine

She pulled a bottle of wine from the rack and opened it.

Liz walked into the dining area and found the table set for two and with hors d'oeuvres waiting.

"How'd this happen? We were out all day?" said Liz.

"Nichol took care of arranging this. You've been working hard, and he knows this is the last evening we have together. He wanted to do this for us, so we could spend time together, pack and enjoy ourselves. He's an exceptional man," said Sabine.

"I agree. I'm happy for you Sabine!"

Liz and Sabine enjoyed their last evening together, laughing, sharing a bottle of wine, enjoying the food Nichol had arranged for them when Sabine surprised Liz with one more gift.

"I thought you might need a larger suitcase."

Liz protested.

"I have two suitcases and that's all my flight allows."

"You can leave the smaller of your two bags here. Then the next time I come to the states, you can send me home with the large suitcase. You and I both know when traveling to a foreign country you always find things unavailable at home and end up needing larger luggage."

Both Liz and Sabine laughed about this and agreed it was true. It amazed Liz. Using the luggage Sabine gave her with one piece she brought with her everything fit into the two pieces of luggage. They hugged and said good night.

The next morning, Liz and Sabine rushed down to the bakery to pick up two lattes to go and a couple pastries. Liz said her goodbyes and hugged everyone before heading out to Sabine's car.

On the way to the airport, Liz was unusually silent. She watched the scenery pass by, knowing it'd be a long time before she'd see these sights again.

"My, you're quiet today. Is everything okay?" said Sabine.

Liz said, "I'm glad I came to Paris. This trip has been amazing! It's hard to imagine it coming to an end. I'll miss you and this neighborhood. Everyone here has treated me like I belong. Yet I'm also looking forward to being with Eric."

"Travel can do that to a person. You love many of the new sights and experiences in a different culture. Yet you long for the comfort of home and what's familiar. I don't plan on letting our friendship slip away again," said Sabine.

"Good. I don't want to lose our friendship either."

The rest of the ride to the airport was rather quiet. Sabine parked the car and helped Liz get her luggage into Terminal 1. Liz checked in; they hugged again and said their goodbyes then Liz stepped on the escalator. She looked back and saw Sabine standing there; they exchanged goodbye kisses and waves.

Liz boarded her plane and found her seat. As the plane took off Liz's thoughts returned to the Dream Glasses. It was the first time she'd considered them since Eric told her the company cancelled the project. She wondered why the Dream Glasses worked for her when so many people saw nothing. Some time before she drifted off to sleep she realized it didn't matter. She needed something new in her life and the glasses for whatever reason, provided the motivation she needed to make a change.

End

Appendix

Gluten-Free Madeleines

Ingredient List for 24 Madeleines:

3 whole eggs

½ Cup sugar

2 ½ Tablespoons of cold milk

¼ Cup of brown rice flour

¼ Cup of white rice flour

¼ Cup of tapioca flour

¼ Cup of almond flour

1 teaspoon Xantham gum

1 ½ teaspoons of baking powder

½ Cup of hot melted butter

Use metal madeleine molds/trays

Ingredients for the Delicious Orange Citrus Glaze:

  1 Cup of powdered sugar

  ¼ Cup of freshly squeezed orange juice

In a bowl mix the flours and the Xantham gum together thoroughly to ensure all the flours will be equally distributed in the batter.

In another deep bowl (or mixer), first beat the eggs with a whisk, then following the steps below, slowly add each one of the ingredients making sure to whisk in-between each new addition.

Step 1: Add sugar

Step 2: Whisk and "don't be afraid to put your body weight into it."

Step 3: Add milk and whisk…

Step 4: Add flour mixture, baking powder and whisk…

Step 5: Add the hot butter and whisk…

Step 6: Butter the Madeleine mold(s) only lightly. Too much butter in the crevice grooves will keep the dough batter from seeping into the crevices to give the back of the Madeleine that wonderful scallop shape. Cover both the batter and the molds and refrigerate overnight. Refrigerating overnight helps form the bump on the backside of the Madeleine. If you can't refrigerate the pans overnight, you can put the pans in the freezer for about 10 minutes before baking.

Step 7: Generously flour the entire mold, and then slam it sideways onto a counter surface to remove excess. (**NOTE:** With non-stick molds this is not necessary.)

Step 8: Use a spoon to fill each mold in the cookie sheet.

Step 9: Place the molds on a baking sheet and then into a 445°F oven (or 420°F convection oven) for six minutes, before taking the tray out to reinsert it backwards (to ensure even baking) for an additional six minutes. Keep the oven on.

Step 10: As soon as they are done, take them out of the oven and immediately slam the mold sideways to remove the Madeleines, or use a spatula to lift them from the cookie sheet.

Step 11: Place them individually on a cooling rack.

Step 12: Mix the orange juice and sugar. Once the Madeleines are at room temperature, dip the top of the Madeleine surface into the orange glaze mixture.

Step 13: Set aside each on a rack sitting on a baking sheet to catch the drips.

Step 14: Place the rack and baking sheet of glazed Madeleines into the oven for about 2 minute, watching for the glaze "bubbling" on the edges – indicating they are ready to remove and cool.

The result? A golden box of gorgeous light Madeleines – fluffy and moist on the inside, firm and kissed by a touch of orange sweetness on the outside.

Dream Glasses

Thank you for reading *Dream Glasses*. I hope you enjoyed it. If you did, please help other readers find this book:

1. The Kindle version of this book is lendable, so send it to a friend you think might like it so she can discover me, too. (Terms of lending established by "Lending for Kindle.")
2. Help other people find this book by writing a review.
3. Check out my website: journeytotheheights.com
4. Sign up for new releases by using the "Sign Me Up" page on my website. You'll find about the next book as soon as it is available.
5. Come 'like' my Facebook page, Linda Flynn.